Love Comes Softly

Books by Janette Oke

Also look for *Janette Oke: A Heart for the Prairie*
by Laurel Oke Logan

*with Davis Bunn   **with Laurel Oke Logan

Love Comes Softly

JANETTE OKE

BETHANY HOUSE PUBLISHERS
a division of Baker Publishing Group
Minneapolis, Minnesota

© 1979, 2003 by Janette Oke

Published by Bethany House Publishers
11400 Hampshire Avenue South
Bloomington, Minnesota 55438
www.bethanyhouse.com

Bethany House Publishers is a division of
Baker Publishing Group, Grand Rapids, Michigan

Printed in the United States of America

40th Anniversary Edition published 2019

ISBN 978-0-7642-3438-5

The Library of Congress has cataloged the 2003 edition as follows:
Oke, Janette
    Love comes softly / Janette Oke. — Rev. 2003 ed.
    p. cm. — (Love comes softly series ; bk. 1)
    ISBN 0-7642-2832-3 (softcover)
    1. Davis family (fictitious characters : Oke)—Fiction. 2. Women pioneers—Fiction.
    I. Title. II. Series: Oke, Janette, Love comes softly series : bk. 1
PS3565.K35L688 2003
813'.54—dc21   2003001482

Cover design by LOOK Design Studio
Cover photography by Mike Habermann Photography, LLC

19 20 21 22 23 24 25   7 6 5 4 3 2 1

To my dear friend and former teacher,
Mrs. Irene Lindberg

Contents

One

The Grim Reaper

The morning sun shone brightly on the canvas of the covered wagon, promising an unseasonably warm day for mid-October. Marty fought for wakefulness, coming slowly out of a troubled and fitful sleep. Why did she feel so heavy and ill at ease—she who usually woke with enthusiasm and readiness for each new day's adventure? Then it all came flooding back, and she fell in a heap on the quilt from which she had just emerged. Sobs shook her body, and she pressed the covering to her face to muffle the sound.

Clem is gone. The truth of it was nearly unthinkable. Less than two short years ago, strong, adventurous, boyish Clem had quickly and easily made her love him. Self-assured and confident, he had captured her heart and her hand. Fourteen months later, she was a married woman out west, beginning a new and challenging adventure with the man she loved—until yesterday.

Oh, Clem, she wept. Her whole world had fallen around her

when the men came to tell her that Clem was dead. Killed outright. His horse had fallen. They'd had to destroy the horse. Did she want to come with them?

No, she'd stay.

Would she like the missus to come over?

No, she'd manage.

She wondered how she had even gotten the words past her lips.

They'd care for the body, one of them had told her. His missus was right good at that. The neighbors would arrange for the burying. Lucky the parson was paying his visit through the area. Was to have moved on today, but they were certain that he'd stay over. Sure she didn't want to come with them?

No, she'd be all right.

Hated to leave her alone.

She needed to be alone.

They'd see her on the morrow. Not to worry. They'd care for everything.

Thank ya—

And they had gone, taking her Clem with them, wrapped in one of her few blankets and fastened on the back of a horse. The kindly neighbor should have been riding it, but he was now leading the animal slowly, careful of its burden.

And now it was the morrow and the sun was shining. Why was the sun shining? Didn't nature know that today should be as lifeless as she felt, with a cold wind blowing like the chill that gripped her heart?

The fact that she was way out west in the fall of the year with no way back home, no one around that she knew—and she was expecting Clem's baby besides—should have filled her with panic. But for the moment the only thing her mind could settle on and her heart grasp was the overwhelming pain of her great loss.

"Oh, Clem! Clem!" she cried aloud. "What am I gonna do without you?" She buried her face again in the quilt.

Clem had come out west with such wild excitement.

"We'll find everything we want there in thet new country. The land's there fer the takin'," he had exulted.

"What 'bout the wild animals—an' the Injuns?" she had stammered.

He had laughed at her silliness, picked her up in his strong arms, and whirled her around in the air.

"What 'bout a house? It'll be 'most winter when we git there," she worried.

"The neighbors will help us build one. I've heered all 'bout it. They'll help one another do whatever needs to be done out there."

And it was true. Those hardy frontiersmen scattered across the wilderness would leave their highly valued crops standing in the fields, if need be, while they gave of their time to put a roof over a needy if somewhat cocky and reckless newcomer, because they would know far better than he the fierceness of the winter winds.

"We'll make out jest fine. Don't ya worry yourself none, Marty," Clem had assured her. With some reluctance, Marty had begun preparations for the long trek by wagon train to follow her beloved husband's dream.

After many weeks of travel, they had come upon a farmhouse in an area of rolling hills and pastureland, and Clem had made inquiries. Over a friendly cup of coffee, the farmer had informed them that he owned the land down to the creek, but the land beyond that, reaching up into the hills, had not yet been claimed. With an effort, Clem had restrained himself from whooping on the spot. Marty could tell that the very thought of being so near his dream filled Clem with wild anticipation. Thanking their soon-to-be neighbor, they hurried on, traveling a bit too fast for the much-mended wagon. They were within sight of their destination when another wheel gave way, and this time it was beyond repair.

They had camped for the night, still on the neighbor's land, and Clem had piled rocks and timbers under the broken wagon in an effort to make it somewhat level. In the morning they had discovered more bad luck. One of the horses had deserted them during the night, and his broken rope still dangled from the tree. Clem had ridden out on the remaining horse to look for it. And then the accident, and now he wouldn't be coming back. There would be no land claimed in his name, nor a house built that would stand proud and strong to shelter his wife and baby.

Marty sobbed again, but then she heard a noise outside the wagon and peeped timidly through the canvas. Neighbors were there—four men with grim faces, silently and soberly digging beneath the largest spruce tree. As she realized what their digging meant, a fresh torment tore at her soul. *Clem's grave.* It was really true. This horrible nightmare was actually happening. Clem was gone. She was without him. He would be buried on borrowed land.

"Oh, Clem. What'll I do?"

She wept until she had no more tears. The digging continued. She could hear the scraping of the shovels, and each thrust seemed to stab deeper into her heart.

More sounds reached her, and she realized that other neighbors were arriving. She must take herself in hand. Clem would not want her hiding away inside the wagon.

She climbed from the quilt and tried to tidy her unruly hair. Quickly dressing in her dark blue cotton frock, which seemed to be the most suitable for the occasion, she snatched a towel and her comb and slipped out of the wagon and down to the spring to wash away her tears and straighten her tangled hair. This done, she squared her shoulders, lifted her chin, and went back to meet the somber little group gathered under the spruce.

There was a kindness, a caring, in all of them. She could feel it. It was not pity, but an understanding. This was the West. Things were hard out here. Most likely every person there had faced a similar time, but one didn't go under. There was no time or energy for pity here—not for self, not for one another. It took your whole being to accept the reality that death was part of life, that the sorrow was inevitable, but that you picked up and carried on.

The visiting pastor spoke the words of interment, committing Clem's body to the dust of the earth, his soul into the hands of God. He also spoke to the sorrowing, who in this case was one lone, small person, the widow of the deceased; for one could hardly count the baby that she was carrying as one of the mourners, even if it was Clem's.

Pastor Magnuson spoke words that were fitting for the occasion—words of comfort and words of encouragement. The neighbors listened in silent sympathy to the familiar Scriptures they had heard on similar occasions. When the brief ceremony was over, Marty, her head bowed, turned from the grave toward the wagon, and the four men with the shovels went back to the task of covering the stout wooden box they had brought with them. As Marty walked away, a woman stepped forward and placed her hand on the slim shoulder.

"I'm Wanda Marshall," she said, her voice low. "I'm sorry we don't have any more than the one room, but you'd be welcome to share it for a few days until you sort things out."

"Much obliged." Marty spoke in almost a whisper. "But I wouldn't wanta impose upon ya. 'Sides, I think I'll jest stay on here fer a while. I need me time to think."

"I understand," the woman answered with a small pat, and she moved away.

Marty continued toward the wagon and was stopped again, this time by an older woman's gentle hand.

"This ain't an easy time fer ya, I know. I buried my first husband many years ago, and I know how you're feelin'." She paused a minute and then went on. "I don't s'pose you've had ya time to plan." At the slight shake of Marty's head, she continued, "I can't offer ya a place to stay; we're full up at our place. But I can offer ya somethin' to eat, and iffen you'd like to move yer wagon to our yard, we'd be happy to help ya pack yer things, and my Ben, Ben Graham, will be more'n glad to help ya git to town whenever yer ready to go."

"Thank ya," Marty murmured, "but I think I'll stay on here fer a while."

How could she explain that she had no money to stay, not even for one night, and no hope of getting any? What kind of work could a young, untrained woman in her condition hope to get? What kind of a future was there for her, anyway?

Her feet somehow moved her on to the wagon and she lifted a heavy hand to the canvas flap. She just wanted to crawl away, out of sight, and let the world cave in upon her.

It was hot in there at midday, and the rush of torrid air sent her already dizzy head to spinning. She crawled back out and down on the grass on the shady side of the wagon, propping herself up against the broken wheel. Her senses seemed to be playing tricks on her. Round and round in her head swept the whirlwind of grief, making her wonder what truly was real and what imagined. She was mentally groping to make some sense of it all when a male voice suddenly made her jump with its closeness.

"Ma'am."

She lifted her head and looked up. A man stood before her, cap in hand, fingering it determinedly as he cleared his throat. She vaguely recognized him as one of the shovel bearers. His height and build evidenced strength, and there was an oldness about his eyes that belied his youthful features. Her eyes looked into his face, but her lips refused to respond.

He seemed to draw courage from somewhere deep inside himself and spoke again.

"Ma'am, I know thet this be untimely—ya jest havin' buried yer husband an' all. But I'm afraid the matter can't wait none fer a proper-like time an' place."

He cleared his throat again and glanced up from the hat in his hands.

"My name be Clark Davis," he hurried on, "an' it 'pears to me thet you an' me be in need of one another."

A sharp intake of breath from Marty made him pause, then raise a hand.

"Now, hold a minute," he told her, almost a command. "It jest be a matter of common sense. Ya lost yer man an' are here alone." He cast a glance at the broken wagon wheel, then crouched down to speak directly to her.

"I reckon ya got no money to go to yer folks, iffen ya have folks to go back to. An' even if thet could be, ain't no wagon train fer the East will go through here 'til next spring. Me, now, I got me a need, too."

He stopped there and his eyes dropped. It was a minute before he raised them and looked into her face. "I have a little 'un, not much more'n a mite—an' she be needin' a mama. Now, as I see it, if we marries, you an' me"—he looked away a moment, then faced her again—"we could solve both of those problems. I would've waited, but the preacher is only here fer today an' won't be back through agin 'til next April or May, so's it has to be today."

He must have recognized in her face the sheer horror Marty was feeling.

"I know. I know," he stammered. "It don't seem likely, but what else be there?"

What else indeed? raged through Marty's brain. *I'd die first, that's all. I'd rather die than marry you—or any man. Get out. Go away.*

But he didn't read any more of her rampaging thoughts and went on. "I've been strugglin' along, tryin' to be pa an' ma both fer Missie, an' not doin' much of a job of it, either, with tryin' to work the land an' all. I've got me a good piece of land an' a cabin thet's right comfortable like, even if it be small, an' I could offer ya all the things thet a woman be a needin' in exchange fer ya takin' on my Missie. I be sure thet ya could learn to love her. She be a right pert little thing." He paused. "But she do be needin' a woman's hand, my Missie. That's all I be askin' ya, ma'am. Jest to be Missie's mama. Nothin' more. You an' Missie can share the bedroom. I'll take me the lean-to. An' . . ." He hesitated a bit. "I'll promise ya this, too. When the next wagon train goes through headin' east to where ya can catch yerself a stagecoach, iffen ya ain't happy here, I'll see to yer fare back home—on one condition—thet ya take my Missie along with ya." He paused to swallow, then said, "It jest don't be fair to the little mite not to have a mama."

He rose suddenly. "I'll leave ya to be a thinkin' on it, ma'am. We don't have much time."

He turned and strode away. The sag of his shoulders told her how much the words had cost him. Still, she thought angrily, what kind of a man could propose marriage—even this kind of a marriage—to a woman who had just turned from her husband's grave? She felt despair well up within her. *I'd rather die*, she told herself. *I'd rather die*. But what of Clem's baby? She didn't want death for their little one, neither for her sake nor for Clem's. Frustration and anger and grief whirled through her. What a situation to be in. No one, nothing, out in this Godforsaken country. Family and friends were out of reach, and she was completely alone. She knew he was right. She needed him, and she hated him for it.

"I hate this country! I hate it! I hate him, the cold, miserable man! I hate him! I hate him!" But even as she stormed against him, she knew she had no way around it.

She wiped her tears and got up from the shady grass. She wouldn't wait for him to come back in his lordly fashion for her decision, she thought stubbornly, and she went into the wagon and began to pack the few things she called hers.

Two

A Mama for Missie

They rode in silence in his wagon. The preacher was at the Grahams', where he had gone for dinner. Missie was there, too, having been left with the Graham family for the older girls to look after while her pa was at the funeral. They'd have the preacher speak the words, pick up Missie, and then go on to the homestead. Marty sat stiff and mute beside him as the wagon jostled on. She struggled to lift a hand and push breeze-tossed hair back from her hot face. He looked at her with concern in his eyes.

"Won't be too long now. It's powerful hot in the sun. Ya be needin' a bonnet to shade yer head."

She sat silent, looking straight ahead. What did he care about the hot sun on her head? What did she care? Nothing worse could possibly happen to her. She turned her face away so he couldn't see the tears forming against her will. She wanted no sympathy from this stubborn man beside her.

The horses trudged on. Her body ached from the bouncing of the wagon over the track of ruts that had to make do as the road.

She was relieved to see the homestead of the Grahams appear at the base of a cluster of small hills. They drove into the yard, and he leaped lightly down and turned to help her. She was too numb to refuse, fearing that if she tried it on her own, she'd fall flat into the dust. He lifted her down easily and steadied her on her feet before he let her go. He flipped a rein around the hitching post and motioned her to precede him into the house.

She noticed nothing of her surroundings. In her befuddled state, her mind refused to record anything. She remembered only that the door was opened by a surprised Mrs. Graham, who looked from the one to the other. Marty was vaguely aware that others were there, apparently waiting for the call to the midday meal. In the corner she saw the preacher in conversation with a man, who, she supposed, was Ben. Children seemed to be all around. She didn't even try to ascertain how many. The man—Clark Davis, he'd said his name was—moved toward the two men in the corner while he talked to Mrs. Graham.

Including the preacher and Ben in his explanation, he was saying, "We've decided—"

We! she stormed within herself. *Ya mean you.*

". . . to marry up while the preacher be still here to do the honors. It will mean a home fer Mrs. Claridge here an' a mama fer my Missie."

She heard Mrs. Graham's "It's the only sensible thing to be a doin'" and the preacher's "Yes, yes, of course."

There was a general stir about her as a spot was cleared, and in what seemed almost an immorally brief span of time she was hearing the familiar words. She must have uttered her own responses at the proper times, for the preacher's words came through the haze, ". . . now pronounce you man and wife."

There was a stirring about her again. Mrs. Graham was setting extra places at the table and encouraging them to "set up an' eat with us afore ya go on." And then they were at the table. The children must have been fed by the older girls before the grown-ups arrived home from the funeral. The preacher blessed the food, and general talk continued on around her. She probably ate something, though she later could not remember what it was or anything else about the meal. She felt like a puppet, moving, even speaking automatically—being controlled by something quite outside of herself.

They were moving again. Getting up from the table, making preparations to be on their way. The preacher tucked away a lunch that had been prepared for him and said his farewells. One of the older Graham boys led the man's horse up from the barn. Before the preacher left the house, he turned to Marty and in a simple, straightforward manner took her hands in his and wished God to be very near her in the coming months. Marty could only stare dumbly into his face. Ben and Clark followed him to his waiting horse, and Mrs. Graham said her good-bye from the open door. Then he was gone. Mrs. Graham turned back into the room, and the men went toward the hitching rail and Clark's team.

"Sally Anne, ya go an' git young Missie up from her nap an' ready to go. Laura, you an' Nellie clear up the table an' do up these dishes."

Mrs. Graham bustled about, but Marty was aware only of the movement about her as she sat limp and uncaring.

Sally returned, carrying a slightly rumpled little figure, who, in spite of her sleepiness, managed a happy smile. Marty noticed only the smile and the deep blue eyes that looked at her, being a stranger to the little one. *This must be Missie,* she thought woodenly. This was verified when Clark stepped through the door and the girl welcomed him with a glad cry and outstretched arms. He swept her up against his chest and for a moment placed a cheek against hers. Then, thanking his host and hostess, he turned to let Marty know that they'd be on their way.

Mrs. Graham walked out with her. There were no congratulations or well-wishing on the new marriage. No one had made an attempt to make an occasion of it, and Marty breathed a sigh of relief for that. One misplaced word, no matter how sincerely spoken, would have broken her reserve and caused the tears to flow, she was sure. But none had been spoken. Indeed, the marriage was not even mentioned. These pioneer people were sensitive to the feelings of others.

They said good-bye only as one neighbor to another, though Mrs. Graham's eyes held a special softness as she looked up at Marty on the wagon seat and said simply, "I'll 'llow ya a few days to be settlin' in an' then I'll be over. It'll be right nice to have another woman so close to hand to visit now an' then."

Marty thanked her and the team moved forward. They were again at the mercy of the dusty road and the hot sun.

"There it be—right over there." Marty almost jumped at Clark Davis's words, but she lifted her eyes to follow his pointing finger.

Sheltered by trees on the north and a small rise on the west was the homestead that belonged to this man beside her.

A small but tidy cabin stood apart, with a well out front and a garden spot to one side. A few small bushes grew along the path to the door, and even from the distance Marty could see colors of fall blooms among their stems.

Off to one side was a sturdy log barn for the horses and cattle, and a pig lot stood farther back among a grove of trees. There was a chicken house between the barn and the house and various other small buildings scattered here and there. She supposed she must learn all about each of them, but right now she was too spent to care.

"It's nice," she murmured, surprising herself, for she hadn't intended to say any such thing. Somehow, in her mind, it looked so much like the dreams that she and Clem had shared, and the knowledge hurt her and made her catch her breath in a quiet little sob. She said nothing more and was relieved when Missie, seeing that they were home, took all of her pa's attention in her excitement.

When they pulled up at the front of the cabin, a dog came running out to meet them and was greeted affectionately by both Clark and Missie.

Clark helped Marty down and spoke gently. "Ya best git ya in out of the sun and lay yerself down a spell. Ya'll find the bedroom off'n the sittin' room. I'll take charge of Missie an' anythin' else thet be needin' carin' fer. It's too late to field work today anyway."

He opened the door and held it while she passed into this strange little house that was to be her home, and then he was gone, taking Missie with him.

She didn't take time to look around her. Feeling that she must lie down or else collapse, she made her way through the kitchen and found the door off the sitting room that led to the bedroom. The bed looked inviting, and she stopped only long enough to slip her feet from her shoes before falling upon it. It was cooler in the house, and her weary body began to demand first consideration over her confused mind. Sobs overtook her, but gradually her churning emotions subsided enough to allow her to sink into deep but troubled sleep.

Three

Marriage of Convenience

Marty awoke and stared toward the window, surprised to see it was already dusk. Vaguely aware of someone stirring about in the kitchen, the smell of coffee and bacon made her acknowledge she was hungry. She heard Missie's chatter, and the realization of why she was here swept over her again. Without caring about anything, she arose, slipped on her shoes, and pushed her hair back from her face. She supposed she looked a mess, but what did it matter? She was surprised in the dim light to see her trunk sitting against the wall by a chest of drawers. Everything she owned was in there, but that thought failed to stir her.

She opened the trunk, took out her brush, and stroked it over her hair. Then she rummaged for a ribbon and tied her hair back from her face. She had made some improvement, she hoped. She smoothed her wrinkled dress and moved toward the bedroom door and the smell of the coffee. Clark looked at her inquiringly as she entered the room, then motioned her to a chair at the table.

"I'm not much of a cook," he said, "but it be fillin'."

Marty sat down and Clark came from the stove with a plate of pancakes and another with a side of bacon. He set it down and went back for the steaming coffee. She felt a sense of embarrassment as she realized he was taking up what she should have been doing. Well, it would be the last time. From now on she'd carry her load. Clark sat down, and just as Marty was about to help herself to a pancake, she was stopped by his voice.

"Father, thank ya fer this food ya provide by yer goodness. Be with this, yer child, as Comforter in this hour, an' bless this house an' make it a home to each one as dwells here. Amen."

Marty sat wide-eyed looking at this man before her, who spoke, eyes closed, to a God she did not see or know—and him not even a preacher. Of course she had heard of people like that, various ones who had a God outside of church, who had a religion apart from marryin' an' buryin', but she had never rubbed elbows, so to speak, with one before. Nor did she wish to now, if she stopped to think about it. So he had a God. What good did it do him? He'd still needed someone to help with his Missie, hadn't he? His God didn't seem to do much about that. Oh well, what did she care? If she remembered right, people who had a God didn't seem to hold with drinkin' an' beatin' their women. With a little luck she maybe wouldn't have to put up with anything like that. A new wave of despair suddenly overwhelmed her. She knew nothing about this man. Maybe she should be glad that at least he was religious. It might save her a heap of trouble.

"Ain't ya hungry?"

His words made her jump, and she realized she had been sitting there letting her thoughts wander.

"Oh yeah, yeah," she stammered and helped herself to the pancake he was holding out to her.

Little Missie ate with a hearty appetite, surprising in one so tiny, and chattered to her father at the same time. Marty thought she picked out a word or two here and there, but she really couldn't put her mind to understanding what the child was saying.

After the meal she heard herself volunteering to wash up the dishes, and Clark said fine, he'd see to putting Missie to bed, then. He showed Marty where things were and then, picking up Missie, he began washing and readying her for bed.

Marty set to work on the dishes. As she opened doors and drawers of another woman's cupboards, a further sense of uneasiness settled on her. She must force herself to get over this feeling, she knew, for she had to manage in this as if it belonged to her. She couldn't restrain the slight shudder that ran through her, though.

As she returned from emptying her dishwater on the rosebush outside the door, Clark was pulling a chair up to the kitchen table.

"She be asleep already," he said quietly.

Marty placed the dishpan on its peg and hung the towel on the rack to dry. *What now?* she wondered in panic, but he took care of that for her.

"The drawers in the chest all be empty. I moved my things to the lean-to. Ya can unpack an' make yerself more comfortable like. Feel free to be a usin' anythin' in the house, an' if there be anythin' thet ya be needin', make a list. I go to town most Saturdays fer supplies, an' I can be a pickin' it up then. When ya feel more yerself like, ya might want to come along

26

an' do yer own choosin'." He paused a moment, then looked into her face.

"I think thet ya better git ya some sleep," he said, his voice low. "It's been a tryin' day. I know thet it's gonna take ya some time before it stops hurtin' so bad—fer ya to feel at home here. We'll try not to rush ya."

Then his gaze demanded that she listen and understand. "I married ya only to have Missie a mama. I'd be much obliged if ya 'llow her to so call ya."

It was an instruction to her; she could feel it as such. But her eyes held his steadily, and though she said nothing, her pride challenged him. All right, she knew her place. He offered her an abode and victuals; she in turn was to care for his child. She'd not ask for charity. She'd earn her way. Missie's mama she would be. She turned without a word and made her way to the bedroom. She closed the door behind her and stood for a few moments leaning against it. When she felt more composed, she crossed quietly to look down on the sleeping child. The lamp gave a soft glow, making the wee figure in the crib appear even smaller.

"All right, Missie," Marty whispered, "let's us make ourselves a deal. Ya be a good kid, an' I'll do my best to be a carin' fer ya."

The child looked so tiny and helpless there, and Marty realized that here was someone barely more than an infant whom life had already hurt. What deserving thing had this little one done to have the mother she loved taken from her? Marty's own baby stirred slightly within her, and she placed a hand on the spot that was slowly swelling for the world to know that she was to be a mother. *What if it were my little one, left without my care?* The thought made near terror take hold of her. Again she looked at the sleeping child, the brown curls framing her pixie face, and something stirred within Marty's heart. It wasn't love that she felt, but it was a small step in that direction.

Marty was up the next morning as soon as she heard the soft click of the outside door. Clark must have come into the kitchen before going to the barn. Quietly she dressed so as not to disturb Missie and left the room, determined to uphold her part of the "convenience" marriage which was now her lot. So she had a roof over her head. She'd earn it. She would be beholden to no man, particularly this distant, aloof individual whose name she now shared. She refused, even in her thoughts, to recognize him as her husband. And speaking of names, she cautioned herself, it wasn't going to be easy to remember that she was no longer Martha Claridge but Martha Davis. Listlessly she wondered if there was a legal difficulty if she stubbornly clung to her "real" name. Surely she could be Martha Lucinda Claridge Davis without breaking any laws. Then with a shock she realized her baby would have the Davis name, too.

"Oh no!" She stopped and put her hands to her face. "Oh no, please. I want my baby to have Clem's name," she whispered her horror.

But even as she fought it and the hot tears squeezed out between her fingers, she knew she'd be the loser here, as well. She was in fact married to this man, no matter how unwelcome the idea; and the baby who would be born after the marriage would be his in name, even though Clem was the true father. She felt a new reason to loathe him.

"Well, anyway, I can name my baby Claridge iffen I want to," she declared hotly. "He can't take thet from me."

She brushed her tears on her sleeve, set her chin stubbornly, and moved into the kitchen.

The fire was already going in the big black cook stove. That must have been what he came in for, and Marty was glad she wouldn't have to struggle with that on top of her almost insurmountable task of just carrying on. She opened the cupboard doors and searched through tightly sealed cans until she found the coffee. She knew where the coffeepot was, she thought thankfully. Hadn't she washed it and put it away herself? There was fresh water in the bucket on a low table near the door, and she had the coffee on in very short order.

"Well, thet's the first step," she murmured to herself. "Now what?"

She rummaged around some more and came up with sufficient ingredients to make a batch of pancakes. At least that she could do. She and Clem had almost lived on pancakes, the reason being that there had been little else available for her to prepare. She wasn't going to find it an easy task to get proper meals, she realized. Her cooking experience had been very limited. Well, she'd learn. She was capable of learning, wasn't she? First she'd have to discover where things were kept in this dad-blame kitchen. Marty rarely used words that could be classed as profane, though she had heard plenty in her young lifetime. She sure felt like turning loose a torrent of them now, though. Instead she chose one of her father's less offensive expressions—about the only one she'd ever been allowed to use.

"Dad-blame!" she exploded again. "What's a body to do?"

Clark would expect more than just pancakes and coffee, she was sure, but what and from where was she to get it?

There seemed to be no end of tins and containers in the cupboards, but they were all filled with other basic ingredients, not anything that could work for breakfast.

Chickens! She'd seen chickens, and where there were chickens there should be eggs. She started out in search of some, through the kitchen door, through the shed that was the entry attached to the kitchen. Then her eye caught sight of a strange contraption at the side of the shed. It looked like some kind of pulley arrangement, and following the rope down to the floor, she noticed a square cut in the floorboards, and one end had a handle attached. Cautiously she approached, wondering if she might be trespassing where she did not belong. Slowly she lifted the trapdoor by the handle. At first she could see nothing; then, as her eyes became more accustomed to the darkness, she picked out what appeared to be the top of a large wooden box. That must be what the pulley and rope were for. She reached for it and began to pull on the ropes, noticing that the box appeared to be moving upward. It took more strength than she had guessed it would, yet she found she could handle it quite nicely.

Slowly the box came into view. She could feel the coolness that accompanied it. At last the box was fully exposed, and she slipped the loop of rope over a hook that seemed to be for that purpose. The front of the box was fitted with a door, mostly comprised of mesh, and inside she could see several items of food. She opened the door and gasped at the abundance of good things. There were eggs in a basket; crocks of fresh cream, milk, and butter; side bacon and ham. On the next shelf were some fresh vegetables and little jars containing preserves and, of all things, she decided after a quick sniff, fresh honey. Likely wild. What a find! She'd have no problem with breakfast now. She took out the side bacon and a few eggs. Then she chose some of the jam and was about to lower the box again when she remembered Missie. The child should have milk to drink as long as it was plentiful, and maybe Clark liked cream for his coffee. She didn't know. In fact, she didn't know much at all about the man.

Carefully she lowered the box again and replaced the trap-door. Gathering up her finds, she returned to the kitchen feeling much better about the prospect of putting breakfast on the table.

The coffee was already boiling, and its fragrance reminded her how hungry she was. She took the dishes from the cupboard and set the table. She'd want the food hot when Clark came in from chores, and she didn't know how long they took him in the mornings.

Four

Morning Encounter

Marty had just turned back to mixing her pancakes when she heard Missie stirring. Best get her up and dressed first, she decided, and she left her ingredients and bowl on the table. As she appeared at the bedroom door, Missie's bright smile above the crib railing faded away, and she looked at Marty with surprise, if not alarm.

"Mornin', Missie," Marty said and lifted the child from the crib to place her on the bed.

"Now, I wonder where yer clothes be?" she asked the child, not really expecting an answer.

They were not in the large chest of drawers, for Marty had already opened each drawer when she unpacked her own things the night before. She looked around the room and spotted a small chest beneath the room's one window. It was Missie's, all right, and Marty selected garments she felt were suitable for that day. Missie did have some sweet little dresses. Her mama must have been a handy seamstress.

Marty returned to the tiny one who, wide-eyed, was watching every move. Marty laid the clothes on the bed and reached for Missie, but as the child realized this stranger was about to dress her, she made a wild grab for her shoes and began screaming.

Marty was sure her shrieks would pale a ghost.

"Now, Missie, stop thet," she scolded, but by now the little girl was howling in either rage or fright, Marty knew not which.

"I wan' Pa," she sobbed.

Marty conceded defeat.

"Hush now, hush," she said, picking up the child. Gathering the clothes against the squirming little body, she carried her to the kitchen, where she placed girl and belongings in a corner. Missie possessively pulled her clothes to her, still sobbing loudly. Marty turned back to the pancakes just as the coffee sputtered and boiled over. She made a frantic grab for the pot, pushing it farther to the back of the stove. She'd put in too much wood, she now realized. The stove was practically glowing with the heat. She looked around for something to clean up the mess, and finding nothing suitable, she went to the bedroom, where she pulled a well-worn garment from her drawer. The thing was not much more than a rag anyway, she decided, and back she went to the kitchen to mop up. Missie howled on. It was to this scene that Clark returned. He looked from the distraught Marty, who had by now added a burned finger to the rest of her frustrations, to the screaming Missie in the corner, still clinging furiously to her clothes.

Marty turned from the stove. She had done the best she could for now. She tossed the soggy, stained garment into the corner and gestured toward Missie.

"She wouldn't let me dress her," she told him, trying to keep her voice even. "She jest set up a howlin' fer her pa."

Marty wasn't sure how she expected Clark to respond, but certainly not as he did.

"I'm a-feared a child's memory is pretty short," he said, so calmly that Marty blinked. "She already be fergettin' what it's like to have a mama."

He moved toward the cupboard, not even glancing Missie's way, Marty noted, lest it encourage her to a fresh burst of tears.

"She'll jest have to learn thet ya be her mama now an' thet ya be in charge. Ya can take her on back to the bedroom an' git her dressed an' I'll take over here." He motioned around the somewhat messy kitchen and the partially prepared breakfast. Then he opened a window to let some of the heat from the roaring stove escape, and he did not look at either Marty or Missie again.

Marty took a deep breath and stooped to scoop up Missie, who reacted immediately with screams like a wounded thing, kicking and lashing out as she was carried away.

"Now, look you," Marty said through clenched teeth, "remember our bargain? I said iffen ya be good, I'd be yer mama, an' this ain't bein' good." But Missie wasn't listening.

Marty deposited her on the bed and was shocked to hear Missie clearly and firmly state between hiccuping sobs, "I . . . wan' . . . Mama."

So she does remember. Marty's cold anger began to slowly melt. Maybe Missie felt the way Marty did about Clark—angry and frustrated. She didn't really blame the little one for crying and kicking. She would be tempted to try it herself had not life already taught her how senseless and futile it would be.

Oh, Missie, she thought, *I knows how ya be feelin'. We'll have to become friends slow like, but first*—she winced—*first, I somehow have ta git ya dressed.*

She arranged the clothes in the order she would need them. There would be no hands to sort them out as she struggled with Missie, she knew. Then she sat down and took the fighting child on her knee. Missie was still throwing a fit. No, now it wasn't fear. Marty could sense that it was sheer anger on the child's part.

"Now, Missie, ya stop it."

Marty's voice was drowned out by the child's, and then Marty's hand smacked hard, twice, on the squirming bottom. Perhaps it was just the shock of it, or perhaps the child was aware enough to realize that she had been mastered. At any rate, her eyes looked wide with wonder and the screaming and squirming stopped. Missie still sobbed in noisy, gulping breaths, but she did not resist again as Marty dressed her.

When the battle was over, the child was dressed, and Marty felt exhausted and disheveled. The two eyed each other cautiously.

"Ya poor mite," Marty whispered and pulled the child close. To her surprise, Missie did not resist but cuddled in Marty's arms, allowing herself to be held and loved as they rocked gently back and forth. How long they sat thus Marty did not know, but gradually she realized the child was no longer sobbing. Detecting the smell of frying bacon coming from the kitchen, she roused herself and used her comb, first on her own unruly hair and then on the child's brown curls. She picked up Missie and returned to the kitchen, dipping a cloth in cool water to wash away the child's tears and also to cool her own face. Clark did not look up. *There he is, doing again what I should be doing,* Marty thought dejectedly as she sat Missie at the table. The pancakes were ready, the eggs fried, the bacon sizzling as he lifted it from the pan. The coffee steamed in their cups, and a small mug of milk sat in front of Missie. There was nothing left to do but to sit down herself. He brought the bacon and sat across from her.

She wouldn't be caught this time. She remembered that he prayed before he ate, so she bowed her head and sat quietly waiting. Nothing happened. Then she heard faint stirrings— like the sound of pages being turned. She stole a quick glance and saw Clark, Bible in hand, turning the pages to find the place he wanted. She could feel the color rising slowly to her cheeks, but Clark did not look up.

"Today we'll read Psalm 121," he said and began the reading.

"'I will lift up mine eyes unto the hills, from whence cometh my help.'"

Marty solemnly wished her help would come from the hills. In fact, she'd take it from any direction. She brought her mind back to catch up to Clark's reading.

"'The Lord is thy keeper: the Lord is thy shade upon thy right hand. The sun shall not smite thee by day, nor the moon by night. The Lord shall preserve thee from all evil: he shall preserve thy soul. The Lord shall preserve thy going out and thy coming in from this time forth, and even for evermore.'"

Gently he laid the book aside on a small shelf close to the table, and then as he bowed his head and prayed, Marty was again caught off guard.

Dad-burn him, she fumed, but then her attention was taken by his words.

"Our God, fer this fine day an' yer blessin's, we thank ya."

Blessin's, thought Marty. *Like a howlin' kid, spilled coffee, an' a burned finger? Blessin's like that I can do without.*

But Clark went on. "Thank ya, Lord, thet the first hard mile with Missie be traveled, an' help this one who has come to be her new mama."

He never calls me by my name when he's talkin' to his God, thought Marty, *always "this one." If his God is able to answer his prayers, I sure hope He knows who he's talkin' 'bout. I need all the help thet I can git.*

Marty heard the rattle of spoon against a bowl and realized her mind had been wandering and she'd missed the rest of the prayer, including the "amen," and still she sat, head bowed. She flushed again and lifted her head, but Clark was fixing Missie's pancake, so her embarrassment went unobserved.

At first breakfast was a quiet meal. Little Missie was probably too spent from her morning struggles to be chatty, and Clark seemed preoccupied. Marty, too, sat with her own thoughts, and most were not very pleasant ones.

What after breakfast? she wondered testily.

First she'd have to do up the dishes, then properly clean the messy stove. Then what? She'd jump at a chance to wash up the few pitiful things that comprised her wardrobe. She'd also like to wash the quilts she had and pack them away in her trunk. She'd need them again when she joined the wagon train going east.

Her mind flitted about, making plans as to how she might repair the few dresses she possessed if she could just find a little bit of cloth someplace. Clark said he went to town on Saturdays. This was Wednesday. She'd have to take stock of the cupboards and have a list ready for him. She stole a glance at him and then quickly looked back at her plate. He certainly did not look like a happy man, she told herself. Brooding almost, one could call it. At any rate, deep thinking, as though trying to sort through something.

Then Missie cut in with a contented sigh and a hearty, "All done, Pa." She pushed her plate forward. The face was transformed.

"Thet's Pa's big girl." He smiled lovingly, and the two shared some chattering that Marty made no effort to follow. Clark rose presently and refilled his coffee cup, offering her more, too. Marty scolded herself for not noticing the empty cup first.

Clark pushed back his plate and took a sip of the hot coffee. Then he looked steadily across at her. She met his gaze, though she found it difficult to do so.

"S'pose ya be at a loss, not knowin' where to find things an' all. I see ya found the cold pit. Good! There be also a root cellar out back. Most of the garden vegetables are already there. Only a few things still be out in the garden. A shelf with cannin's there, too, but ya need a light along to do yer choosin', since it be dark in there. There's also a smokehouse out by the root cellar. Not too much in it right now. We plan on doin' our fall killin' and curin' next week. Two of the neighbors and me works together. There be chickens—fer eggs an' fer eatin'. We try not to get the flock down too low, but there's plenty to spare right now. There won't be fresh meat until it turns colder, 'ceptin' fer a bit of the pork. When the cold weather comes we try an' get some wild game—it keeps then. Sometimes we kill us a steer if we think we be needin' it. There be fish in the crik, too. When the work is caught up I sometimes try my hand at a bit of loafin' an' fishin'. We're not bad off, really."

It was not a boast, simply a statement.

"We have us real good land and the Lord be blessin' it. We've had good crops fer the last four seasons. The herd has built up, too, and the hogs an' chickens are plentiful enough. All the garden truck thet we can use can be growin' right outside the house, an' there's lots of grain in the bins fer seedin'. We has some cash—not much, but enough, an' iffen we do be needin' more, we can always sell us a hog.

"We're better off than a lot of folks, but the neighbors round about here are makin' good, too. Seems as how our move to the West's been a good one. Got me some cuttin's a few years back from a man over acros't the crik. An' in a couple of years, if all goes well, we should have some fruit on 'em. The apples might even be a settin' next year, he tells me. I'm a tellin' ya this so's ya be knowin' the lay o' the land, so to speak. Ya don't need to apologize fer askin' fer what ya be needin', both fer yerself an' fer Missie. We've never been fancy, but we try an' be proper like."

He pushed back from the table after his long speech and stood silently for a moment, as if sorting out in his thinking if there was anything else he should tell her.

"We've got a couple o' good milk cows at present an' another due with an off-season calf, so we have all the milk an' butter we be needin'. There's a good team of horses an' a ridin' horse, too, iffen ever ya want to pay a visit to a neighbor's. Ma Graham be the closest, an' she's 'bout as good company as anybody be a wantin'. I think ya'll find her to yer likin', even if she be some older than you.

"Most of my field work is done fer the fall, but I do have me a little breakin' I aim to do yet, iffen winter holds off awhile. First, though, I plan to spend a few days helpin' one o' the neighbors who ain't through yet. He got 'im a slow start. Plan to go over there today—Jedd Larson—an' give 'im a hand. I'll be asked to stay to dinner with 'em so won't be home 'til chore time. Ya can make yerself to home, an' you an' Missie git to know one another like, an' maybe we won't have any more of those early mornin' fusses."

He turned to Missie then and swung her up easily into his arms. "Ya wanna come with Pa to git ole Dan an' Charlie?"

She assented loudly and the two set off for the barn.

Marty stirred herself. *"No more early mornin' fusses."* Looked like this short statement would be his only reference to the incident. He hadn't seemed to pay much heed at the time, but, she reflected, maybe it had bothered him more than he let on.

She began to clear the table. Clark had told her so much that it seemed difficult to sort it all out at one time. She'd shelve it for now and draw on it later as she had need. She began to make plans for her day.

She'd scout around and find a tub to heat water and then wash clothes and quilts as she had hoped she could. Maybe she'd be able to find a needle and thread and do the much-needed repair work, as well.

By the time she had started on the dishes, Clark was back to deposit Missie with her. He had to work to detach her clinging arms. Missie had by now become used to going everywhere with her pa, and it wasn't going to be easy for the first while to make her understand that things would be different now.

"Pa's got to go now, and yer gonna stay with yer mama. I'll be back later," he explained carefully to her over her sobs. After Clark had left and Missie had finally ceased her crying, Marty put away the last of the dishes and set to work cleaning the stove. That done, she swept up the floor and felt ready to turn to her other plans for the day.

She had never had much practice at keeping a real house, but she was determined she would do a good job of it. Clark was never going to be embarrassed about the home that he lived in as long as she was earning her keep as Missie's mama. As soon as she had her own things in order, she'd turn her attention to the house, which had been a bachelor's quarters for too long. Even though Clark had been better than most in keeping things up, still it wasn't as a woman would have it. Just give her a few days. She'd have things looking homey.

Five

Iffen I Can Jest Stick It Out . . .

By late afternoon Marty had finished washing everything that belonged to her and some of Clark's and Missie's clothes, as well. The day was much cooler than the previous one, she noted with relief. She didn't think she could have tolerated another one like that. This felt more like mid-October, a glorious Indian summer day.

Standing at the clothesline, Marty gazed out toward the west. Far beyond the rolling hills, blue mountains rose in majesty. Was it from those peaks that Clark was seeking the help of his God?

The trees along the hillside were garbed in yellows and reds. Indeed, many of the leaves were already on the ground or being carried southward by a gusty breeze.

It was a beautiful scene, and how happy she would have been to share it with Clem. *If only Clem and I could have had this together*. Her heart ached even more than her tired back as she emptied the water from the washtubs.

Missie was having a nap. Marty was glad to be free of the child for a while—almost as glad as she was that Clark was away for the day. How relieved she had felt at his announcement that morning. Maybe with luck the neighbor's work would keep him away for several days. She hardly dared hope for so much. She had planned to look around the farm today to learn where things were, but she felt far too tired just now. She'd just sneak a few minutes of rest while Missie was still sleeping and then take her scouting trip a little later.

She threw out the last of the rinse water, replaced the tubs on the pegs at the side of the house, and extremely weary, went in to stretch out on her bed. She cried a bit before drowsiness claimed her, but the sleep that followed was the most restful she'd had since Clem had died.

Marty awoke with a start—not sure what had roused her but already sensing that something was amiss. Maybe Missie had cried. She propped herself on one elbow and looked at the crib. No, it wasn't that. Missie wasn't even there. *Missie isn't there? But she must be.*

Marty scrambled up, her heart pounding. Where was Missie? Maybe Clark had come home and taken the child out with him.

"Don't panic," she whispered fiercely. "She's got to be somewhere nearby."

Marty checked the little cabin quickly, then the corral, but the team was not back. She looked all around the buildings, calling as she went. No Missie. *She must have climbed right over the crib railing,* she said to herself between shouts for the little girl. *I must have been awfully sound asleep.* Marty ranged farther and farther from the buildings, but still no Missie. She was getting frantic now in spite of her efforts to keep herself under control. Where could Missie be? What should she do?

By now tears were streaming down Marty's cheeks. Her dress had suffered another tear near the hem, and she had thorns in her hands from the wild rosebushes through which she had forced her way. She checked the creek—up and down its banks, searching the clear, shallow water, but no sign of Missie or of anything that belonged to her.

Maybe she followed the road, Marty thought frantically, and she set off at nearly a run down the dusty, rutted roadway. On and on she stumbled. *Surely Missie couldn't have gone this far,* Marty tried to reason, but she hurried on because she knew of nothing else to do. Then over the hill in the road ahead she saw Clark's team coming toward her.

She didn't even consider stopping by the side of the road and waiting for him to approach but plodded doggedly on toward the wagon.

Whatever could she say to Clark? How could she tell him? She could not even be trusted to care for one small child. Would Clark have some idea of where to search that she had not already tried?

Soon she had to step aside to allow the team to draw up beside her. Heart constricting with remorse and fear, she turned her dirt- and tear-streaked face up to Clark—and there sat Missie big as life on her pa's knee, looking very proud of herself.

Clark whoaed the horses to a stop and reached down a hand to help Marty into the wagon. She climbed up reluctantly, her head spinning. *Oh, what must he think?* They traveled toward home in silence. Why didn't he say something? He'd not spoken, other than a giddup to the team. Missie was quiet, too.

Well, she'd better be, the little rascal. If she said one word, Marty knew she'd feel like smacking her. Her great relief at seeing the child safe and sound was now replaced with feelings of anger. Marty's face felt hot, both from the efforts of her frantic search and her deep humiliation. Then her chin went up. So he wasn't talking. Well—neither was she. He could think what he would; she wasn't doing any explaining. She hated him anyway, and she didn't think much more of his undisciplined child.

Iffen I can jest stick it out fer thet wagon train, then I'll be leavin' this wretched place so fast ya won't even find my tracks, she railed silently.

The woman in her wanted desperately to resort to tears, but the woman in her also refused to give in to even that small comfort.

Don't ya dare, she warned herself, *don't ya dare allow him thet satisfaction.*

She held her head high, eyes straight ahead, and remained that way until they reached the house. She disdained any help Clark might have offered and quickly climbed down over the wheel, managing to tear her dress even further.

He placed Missie on the ground, and Marty scooped the child up rather brusquely and went into the house. Missie seemed unaffected by it all and paid no attention as her new mama noisily went about starting another fire in the kitchen stove.

Another meal to prepare—but what? It caused her additional embarrassment, but Marty knew it would have to be pancakes again. That was about the only thing she really knew how to make. Well, let him choke on them. She didn't care. Why should she? She owed him nothing. She wished she had stayed in her wagon and starved to death. That's what she wished.

Amazingly enough, Marty's fire took, and the fine cook stove was soon spilling out heat. Marty didn't even think to be grateful as she stormed about the kitchen, making coffee and preparing the second batch of pancake batter for the day. She'd fry a few pieces of ham rather than bacon, she swiftly decided.

She really couldn't understand why it bothered her so much that all her efforts since coming to this house had met with such complete failure. She shouldn't care at all, and yet she did—much as she didn't want to acknowledge it. Marty felt deeply that failure was a foe to be combated and defeated. It was the way she had grown up, and it was not easily forsaken now.

While the griddle was heating, she cast an angry look at Missie.

"Now, you stay put," she warned, then hurried out to bring in all her washing before the night's dampness set in.

When Clark came in from the barn, supper, such as it was, was ready. If he was surprised at pancakes again, he did not show it. Marty's cheeks again burned to realize that his pancakes had been just as good as hers.

So what? she raged to herself. *My coffee be a sight better.*

It must have been, because when she again missed noticing Clark's empty cup and he got up to refill it, he remarked, "Good coffee," as he poured her a second cup. Marty turned her face away and simply shrugged.

After supper she cleared the table and washed Missie up for bed. She still felt like shaking the little tyke each time she touched her but refrained from doing so.

When Missie had been tucked in and Marty had washed her own hot, dusty feet, she excused herself with a murmur. Gathering her clothes she had brought in from the line, she took the items to her bedroom and shut the door. She carefully folded her worn but clean dresses and undergarments, laying them on her bed. If only she had a needle and some thread. But she wouldn't ask him, she determined. Never!

She sat down on the bed to allow herself time for some well-earned self-pity. It was then she noticed a small sewing basket in the corner behind the door. For a moment she couldn't believe her amazing find, but upon crossing to the basket, she discovered far more than she had dared to hope.

There were threads of various colors, needles of several sizes, a perfect pair of scissors, and even some small pieces of fabric.

Determinedly Marty settled down. Sewing—now, that was one thing she could do. Though mending hardly fit into the same category as sewing, she felt a surge of anticipation.

She was soon dismayed, though, as she tried to make something decent out of the worn things before her. The longer she worked the more discouraged she became. She had attacked the least-worn items first, but by the time she reached the last few articles, she was completely dejected. They'd never last the winter, and it was a sure thing she'd never ask him for anything. Even if she was forced to wear nothing but rags.

"We've never been fancy, but we try an' be proper," she remembered him saying.

"Well, Mr. Proper, what would ya do if ya had nothin' to make yerself proper with?" she demanded through gritted teeth as she pulled the tattered dress over her head and replaced it with a carefully mended nightdress.

Marty fell into bed, and the events of the day crowded through her mind—the too-hot stove and the coffee boiling over, the tantrum-throwing Missie, the frantic search for the child, more pancakes. A sob arose in her throat. *If only Clem were here . . .* and again she cried herself to sleep.

Six

Housecleaning

The next morning presented a cloudy face as Marty looked toward the window. The weather was changing. It wouldn't be long until the beautiful Indian summer would give way to winter's fury. *But not yet,* she told herself, determined to be cheerful in spite of her wretched circumstances. The day was still warm and the sky not too overcast. Perhaps the clouds would soon move away and let the sun shine again.

Slowly she climbed from bed. Surely today must be an improvement on yesterday, she hoped. Already yesterday seemed a long way in the past—and the day before, the day she had buried Clem. Marty could hardly believe it was only two days ago. But two days that had seemed forever.

Marty slipped into the gingham she had mended the night before, cast a glance in Missie's direction, and quietly moved toward the door. She did hope that the morning scene of yesterday would not be repeated. She didn't know if she could face it again.

She put on the coffee and set the dishes on the table, then started preparations for the morning pancakes.

Dad-blame it. She bit her lip. *I'm tired of pancakes myself.*

It hadn't seemed so bad to have pancakes over and over when that was all that was available, but with so many good, fresh provisions at her disposal, it seemed a shame to be eating pancakes. She'd have to figure something out, but in the meantime they needed a meal to start the day. She went out for another piece of side bacon.

Missie awoke and without incident allowed Marty to dress her. So that battle seemed to have been won! She placed the tot in the homemade chair and pulled it back from the table to keep small fingers from getting into things.

When Clark came in from the barn, the breakfast was ready and Missie was sitting well behaved in her chair. Clothed and in her right mind, Clark's expression seemed to say, though he made no comment, to Marty's relief.

They sat down together at the table, and after the morning reading and prayer, breakfast proceeded with nothing out of the ordinary occurring.

Marty watched surreptitiously for Clark's coffee cup to need a refill, but when she jumped up for the pot he waved it aside.

"I'd like to but I'd better not take time for a second cup this mornin'. The sky looks more like winter every day, an' Jedd still has him some grain out. I'm gonna git on over there as quick as I can"—he hesitated—"but thet's right good coffee."

Marty poured her own second cup and put the pot back. The only thing he could say about her was that she made good coffee. Well, maybe she was lucky—and he was lucky—she could do that much!

Clark stopped at the door and said over his shoulder, "I'll be eatin' my noon meal with the Larsons agin." Then he was gone.

This time Missie's whimpering lasted only a few minutes. Marty's thoughts turned to his parting announcement. "Bet he's tickled pink to be able to have 'im one meal a day to the Larsons. Wouldn't it be a laugh should Mrs. Larson give 'im pancakes?"

In spite of herself Marty couldn't keep a smile from flitting across her face. Then she sat down to leisurely enjoy her second cup of coffee and plan her day.

First she would completely empty and scrub out the kitchen cupboards, and then she'd go on to the rest of the kitchen, including the walls, window, and curtains. By night, she vowed, everything would be shining.

She didn't spend as long over her coffee as she had intended, for she became anxious to begin her activities and see everything fresh and clean.

She hurriedly washed up the dishes and found some things she hoped would keep Missie amused for a while. Then she set to work in earnest. She might lack in a lot of ways, she thought, but she could apply herself to work—and apply herself she did.

By the time the ticking clock on the mantel told her that it was twelve-thirty, the cupboards were all scrubbed and rearranged to suit her own fancy. She had discovered several items, too, like ground corn for muffins and grains for cooked cereals. Maybe breakfast wouldn't always have to be pancakes after all.

She stopped her cleaning to prepare a meal for herself and Missie. Fried ham and a slice of bread with milk to drink satisfied them both. She was glad that milk was plentiful. Along their way west, Clem had fretted that she should be drinking milk for the baby. Now there was milk in abundance, and Clem's boy would be strong when he arrived.

After Marty tucked Missie in for her nap, she set to work again. She felt tired, but under no circumstances would she lie down and give Missie a chance to repeat her performance of yesterday. That little mite must have walked over a mile before she met her pa. At the thought of it Marty felt again the fear and sting of humiliation. No sirree, there was no way she would let that happen again, even if she dropped dead on her feet.

On she worked, washing the curtains and placing them out in the breeze to dry. Then she tackled the window until it shone, and went on to the kitchen walls with more energy than she knew she possessed. It was hard, slow work, but she was pleased with her accomplishment. As she scrubbed away at the wooden log walls, she was amazed at the amount of water it took. A number of times she had to stop and refill her pan. Remembering the curtains, she stopped her scrubbing and went in search of anything resembling an iron so she could press the curtains before rehanging them. She found a set of sad irons in the shed's corner cupboard and placed them on the stove to heat. She then realized that in her preoccupation with her scrubbing, she had let the fire go out, so the task of rebuilding it was hers once more. She scolded herself as she fussed with the small flame to try to coax it into a blaze. When finally it began to sustain itself, she returned to her scrubbing. She refilled her pan many more times and had to take the buckets to the well for more water. Finally the task was finished. The logs shined, even if they had soaked up the water.

By the time she brought in the curtains, the irons were hot

JANETTE OKE

enough to press them. The renewed curtains looked fresh and crisp as she placed them at the window.

Missie wakened and Marty brought her from her bed and got a mug of milk for each of them. Missie seemed cheerful and chatty after her sleep, and Marty found her talkative little companion rather enjoyable. It kept her mind off other things—just as her hard work had been doing.

She placed Missie in her chair with a piece of bread to nibble on and set to work on the wooden floor with hot soapy water and scrub brush. By the time she was through, her arms and back ached, but the floor was wondrously clean. She gave the rug at the door a good shaking outside and replaced it again, then stood and surveyed the small kitchen. Everything looked and smelled clean. She was proud of herself. The kitchen window gleamed, the curtains fairly crackled with crispness, the walls—well, now, the walls looked sort of funny. Oh, the logs looked clean and shiny but the chinking—somehow the chinking looked strange, sort of gray and muddy instead of the white it had been before.

Marty crossed to the nearest wall and poked a finger at the chinking. It didn't just look muddy. It *was* muddy—muddy and funny. Marty wrinkled her nose. What had she done? The water, of course! It wasn't the logs that had drunk up the water; it was the chinking! It had slurped up the scrub water thirstily and was now gooey and limp. She hoped with all of her heart that it would dry quickly before Clark got home. She looked at the clock. It wouldn't be long, either. She'd better get cracking if supper was to be more than pancakes.

She had noticed that the bread was as good as gone. Then what would she do? She had never baked bread before, nor even

53

watched her mother do it that she could remember. She hadn't the slightest idea how to start. Well, she'd make biscuits. She didn't know how to bake them, either, but surely it couldn't be too hard. She washed her hands and went to the cupboard. She felt that it was more "her" cupboard now that she had put everything where she wanted it.

She found the flour and salt. Did you put eggs in biscuits? She wasn't sure, but she'd add a couple just in case. She added milk and stirred the mixture. Would that do it? Well, she'd give it a try.

She sliced some potatoes for frying and got out some ham. She supposed that she should have a vegetable, too, so she went to work on some carrots. As she peeled them she heard Ole Bob welcome home the approaching team. Clark would care for the horses and then do the chores. He'd be in for supper in about forty minutes, she guessed, so she left the carrots and went to put the biscuits in the oven. They handled easily enough, and she pictured an appreciative look in Clark's eyes as he reached for another one.

She went back to her potatoes in the frying pan, stirring them carefully so they wouldn't burn.

"Oh, the coffee!" she suddenly cried and hurried to get the coffeepot on to boil. After all, she could make good coffee!

She sliced some ham and placed it in the other frying pan, savoring the aroma as it began to cook. She smelled the biscuits and could barely refrain from opening the oven door to peek at them. She was sure they'd need a few minutes more. She stirred the potatoes again and looked anxiously at the muddy chinking between the logs. It wasn't drying very fast. Well, she wouldn't mention it and maybe Clark wouldn't notice it. By morning it would be its old white self again.

The ham needed turning and the potatoes were done. She pulled them toward the back of the stove and put more wood in the firebox. Then she remembered the carrots. Oh dear, they were still in the peeling pan, only half ready. Hurriedly she went to work on them, nicking a finger in her haste. Finally she had the pot of carrots on the stove, on what she hoped was the hottest spot to hurry them up.

The potatoes were certainly done, rather mushy looking from being overcooked and overstirred, and now they sat near the back of the stove looking worse every minute. The biscuits! Marty grabbed fiercely at the oven door, fearing that the added minutes may have ruined her efforts, but the minutes had not ruined them at all. Nothing could have done any harm to those hard-looking lumps that sat stubbornly on the pan looking like so many rocks.

Marty pulled them out and dumped one on the cupboard to cool slightly before she made the grim test. She slowly closed her teeth upon it—to no avail; the biscuit refused to give. She clamped down harder; still no give.

"Dad-burn," murmured Marty, and opening the stove, she threw the offensive thing in. The flames around it hissed slightly, like a cat with its back up, but the hard lump refused to disappear. It just sat and blackened as the flame licked around it.

"Dad-blame thing. Won't even burn," she stormed and crammed a stick of wood on top of it to cover up the telltale lump.

"Now, what do I do with these?"

Marty looked around. How could she get rid of the lumpy things? She couldn't burn them. She couldn't throw them out to the dog to be exposed to all eyes. She'd bury them. The rotten things. She hurriedly scooped them into her apron and started for the door.

"Missie, ya stay put," she called. Then remembering her previous experience, she turned and pulled the coffeepot to the back of the stove.

Out the door she went, first looking toward the barn to make sure that her path was clear. Then she quickly ran to the far end of the garden. The soil was still soft, and she fell on her knees and hurriedly dug a hole with her hands and dumped in the disgusting lumps. She covered them quickly and sprinted back to the house. When she reached the yard, she could smell burning ham.

"Oh no!" she cried. "What a mess!"

She washed her hands quickly at the outside basin, and the tears washed her cheeks as she raced for the tiny kitchen, where everything seemed to be going wrong.

When Clark came in for supper, he was served lukewarm mushy potatoes and slightly burned slices of ham along with the few slices of bread that remained. There was no mention of the carrots, which had just begun to boil, and of course no mention of the sad lumps called biscuits. Clark said nothing as he ate. Nothing, that is, except, "That's right good coffee."

Seven

A Welcome Visitor

Friday dawned clear and bright again, though the air did not regain the warmth of the first part of the week. Marty lay in bed remembering their supper the night before. She had carefully avoided any comment on the muddy chinking, but one small chunk in the corner had suddenly given way. It lost its footing between the logs, falling to the floor and leaving a bit of a smear on the way down. Clark had looked up in surprise but then had gone on eating. Marty prayed, or would have prayed had she known how, that the rest of it would stay where it dadburn belonged. It did, and she thankfully cleared the table and washed the dishes.

Lamplight was needed in the evenings, as the days were short. The men worked in the fields as late as they could before turning to chores, so it was full dark before supper was over. Marty was glad when darkness had fallen that night. The lamplight cast shadows, obscuring the grayish chinking. As she washed Missie up before bed, she thought she heard another small piece give way, but she refused to acknowledge it, raising her voice to talk to Missie and try to cover the dismaying sound.

That had been last night, and now as Marty tried to prepare herself to face another day, she wondered what new and dreadful things it held for her. One thing she had already confronted. The bread crock was empty, and she had no idea of how to go about restocking it. She supposed Clark knew how to bake bread, but she'd die before she'd ask him. And what about the chinking? Had the miserable stuff finally dried to white and become what it was supposed to be? She dreaded the thought of going to look, but lying there wasn't going to solve any problems.

She struggled up from her bed. Her muscles still ached from her strenuous efforts of the day before. She'd feel it for a few days, she was sure. Besides, she hadn't slept well. Her thoughts had again been on Clem and how much she missed him. Now she dressed without caring, ran a comb through her hair, and went to the kitchen.

The first thing she noticed was the chinking. Here and there all around the walls, small pieces lay crumbled on the floor. Marty felt like crying, but little good that would do. She'd have to face Clark with it, confess what she had done, and accept her well-deserved rebuke for it.

She stuffed a couple of sticks into the fire and put on the coffee. Suddenly she wondered just how many pots of coffee she would have to make in her future. At the moment those pots seemed to stretch into infinity.

She found a kettle and put on some water to boil. This morning they'd have porridge for breakfast. *But porridge and what?* she wondered crossly. What did you have with porridge if you had no biscuits, no muffins, no bread, "no nuthin'," Marty fretted out loud. Pulling the pot off the stove in disgust, she went to work again making pancakes.

Missie awakened and Marty went in to pick her up. The child smiled and Marty found herself returning it.

"Mornin', Missie. Come to Mama," she said, trying the words with effort to see how they'd sound. She didn't really like them, she decided, and wished she hadn't even used them.

Missie came gladly and chattered as she was being dressed. Marty could understand more of the baby words now. She was saying something about Pa, and the cows that went *moo,* and the chickens that went *cluck,* and pigs—Marty couldn't catch the funny sound that represented the pigs, but she smiled at the child as she carried her to her chair.

Clark came in to a now-familiar breakfast and greeted his daughter, who squealed a happy greeting in return.

After the reading of the Bible passage, they bowed their heads for Clark's prayer. He thanked his Father for the night's rest and the promise of "a fair day for the layin' in of the rest of Jedd's harvest."

Marty was surprised at the next part of the prayer.

"Father, be with the one who works so hard to be a proper mama for Missie an' a proper keeper of this home."

The prayer continued, but Marty missed it. Everything she had done thus far had been a failure. No wonder Clark felt it would take help from the Almighty himself to set things in order again. She didn't know if she should feel pleased or angry at such a prayer, so she forcefully shoved aside the whole thing just in time for the "amen."

"Amen," echoed Missie, and breakfast began.

At first they ate rather silently, only Clark and Missie exchanging some comments and Clark scolding Missie.

"Don't ya be a throwin' pancake on the floor. Thet's a naughty girl an' makes more work fer yer mama."

Marty caught a few other references to "yer mama," as well, and realized that Clark had been using the words often in the past two days. She knew he was making a conscious effort at educating the little girl to regard her as mama. She supposed she'd have to get used to it. After all, that's what she was here for—certainly not to amuse the serious-looking young man across the table from her.

Another piece of chinking clattered down, and Marty took a deep breath and burst forth with, "I'm afeared I made a dreadful mistake yesterday. I took to cleanin' the kitchen—"

"I'd seen me it was all fresh and clean lookin' an' smellin'," Clark said quickly.

Now, why'd he do that? she stormed inwardly. She took another gulp of air and went on, "But I didn't know what scrub water would be doin' to the chinkin'. I mean, I didn't know thet it would all soak up like an' then not dry right agin."

Clark said nothing.

She tried once more. "Well, it's fallin' apart like. I mean—well, look at it. It's crumblin' up an' fallin' out—"

"Yeah," said Clark with a short nod, not even lifting his eyes.

"Well, it's not stayin' in place," Marty floundered. "Whatever can we do?"

She was almost angry by now. His calmness unnerved her.

He looked up then and answered slowly. "Well, when I go to town on Saturday, I'll pick me up some more chinkin'. It's a special kind like. Made to look whiter an' cleaner, but no good at all fe___in' out the weather—the outside chinkin' has to do thet ___ There still be time to redo it 'fore winter sets in. Water don't hurt the outer layer none, so it's holdin' firm like. Don't ya worry yerself none 'bout it. I'm sure thet the bats won't be a flyin' through the cracks afore I git to 'em."

He almost smiled and she could have gleefully kicked him. He rose to go.

"I reckon ya been pushin' yerself pretty hard, though, an' it might be well if you'd not try to lick the whole place in a week like. There's more days ahead, an' ya be lookin' kinda tired." He hesitated. "Iffen ya should decide to do more cleanin', jest brush down the walls with a dry brush. All right?"

He kissed Missie good-bye after telling her to be a good girl for her mama and went out the door for what he said might be the last day of helping Jedd Larson with his crop. Marty supposed he'd be around the place more then. She dreaded the thought, but it was bound to come sooner or later.

She put water on to heat so she could wash up the rag rugs before winter set in and then found a soft brush to dust the sitting room walls.

It didn't take nearly as long to brush them as it had to scrub the kitchen, and it did take care of the cobwebs and dust. She was surprised to be done so quickly and went on to the windows and floor, as well.

The sitting room curtains were still fluttering in the fall breeze and the rugs drying in the sun when she heard the dog announce a team approaching. Looking out of the window, she recognized Mrs. Graham, and her heart gave a glad flutter as she went out to welcome her. They exchanged greetings, and Ma Graham put her team in the shade and gave them some hay

to keep them content with the wait. Then ~~er hold~~ ~~Marty~~
to the house. ~~job.~~

The dog lay on one side of the path now, chewing hard on a small, bonelike object. Marty saw with dismay that it was one of her biscuits. The dad-blame dog had dug it up. With a flush to her cheeks, she hurried Mrs. Graham on by, hoping the older woman would fail to recognize the lump for what it really was.

As they entered the kitchen, Marty was overcome with shyness. She had never welcomed another woman into her kitchen. She knew not what to do or say, and she certainly had little to offer this visitor in the way of refreshment.

Marty noticed that Ma Graham kept her eyes discreetly away from the crumbled chinking and remarked instead about the well-scrubbed floor.

Marty bustled about self-consciously, stuffing wood in the stove and putting on the coffee. Ma talked easily of weather, of delightful little Missie, whom her girls loved to care for, and the good harvest. Still Marty felt ill at ease. She was thankful when the coffee had boiled and she was able to pour them each a cup. She placed Missie in her chair with a glass of milk and put on the cream and sweetening for Ma in case she used it. With a sinking heart, she realized she didn't have a thing to serve with the coffee—not so much as a crust of bread. Well, the coffee was all she had, so the coffee would have to do.

"I see ya been busy as a bee, fall cleanin'," Ma observed.

"Yeah," responded Marty.

"Nice to have things all cleaned up fer the long days an' nights ahead when a body can't be out much. Them's quiltin' an' knittin' days."

Yeah, that's how she felt.

"Do ya have plenty of rugs fer comfort?"

She was sure they did.

"What 'bout quilts? Ya be needin' any of those?"

No, she didn't think so.

They slowly sipped their coffee. Then Ma's warm brown eyes turned upon her.

"How air things goin', Marty?"

It wasn't the words, it was the look that did it. The expression in Ma's eyes said that she truly cared how things were going, and Marty's firm resolve to hold up bravely went crumbling just like the chinking. Words tumbled over words as she poured out to Ma all about the pancakes, Missie's stubborn outburst, the bread crock being empty, the horrid biscuits, Missie's disappearance, the chinking, the terrible supper she had served the night before, and, finally, her deep longing for the husband whom she had lost so recently. Ma sat silently, her eyes filling with tears. Then suddenly she rose, and Marty was fearful that she had offended the older woman by her outburst.

"Come, my dear," Ma said gently, her tone putting any fear of offense to rest. "You air gonna have ya a lesson in breadmakin'. Then I'll sit me down an' write ya out every recipe thet I can think of. It's a shame what ya've been a goin' through the past few days, bein' as young as ya are an' still sorrowin' an' all, an' if I don't miss my guess"—her kind eyes traveling over Marty's figure—"ya be in the family way, too, ain't ya, child?"

Marty nodded silently, swallowing her tears, and Ma took over, working and talking and finally managing to make Marty feel more worthwhile than she had felt since she had lost her Clem.

After a busy day, Ma departed. She left behind her a sheaf of recipes with full instructions, fresh-baked bread that filled the kitchen with its aroma, a basketful of her own goodies, and a much more confident Marty with supper well in hand.

Marty breathed a short prayer that if there truly was a God up there somewhere, He'd see fit to send a special blessing upon this wonderful woman whom she had so quickly learned to love.

Eight

It's a Cruel World

Saturday dawned clear and cooler. The breakfast of porridge and corn muffins was hurried so Clark might get an early start to town. Marty presented him with the list that Ma Graham had helped her prepare the day before.

"Mind ya," Ma had told her, "in the winter months it be sometimes three or four weeks between the trips we be a takin' to town because of winter storms, an' ya never know ahead which Saturdays ya be missin', so ya al'ays has to be stocked up like."

So the list had turned out to be a lengthy one, and Marty inwardly was concerned, but Clark did not seem surprised as he skimmed quickly through it. He nodded his agreement with the list, then bent to kiss Missie good-bye, promising her a surprise when he returned.

Marty sighed in relief at another day without him about and turned her thoughts to planning what she would do with it. Clark had cautioned her to take things a bit easier, and Ma Graham said she feared that Marty was "overdoin' for a woman in her state," but Marty knew she must have something demanding to fill her hours or the sense of her terrible loss would overwhelm her. She looked around to see what to tackle on this day. She'd finish her cleaning, she decided. First she'd put water on to heat so she could wash the bedding. Then she'd do the window, walls, and floor in the bedroom, and if time still allowed, she'd do the shed. She did not even consider cleaning the lean-to. *That's Clark's private quarters,* she told herself, and she would not intrude.

Setting Missie up with her little rag doll and a small hand-made quilt to wrap it in, Marty began her tasks, forcing her mind to concentrate on what she was doing. A nagging fear raised its head occasionally. If she finished all the hard cleaning today, what would she do tomorrow, and the next day, and the day after that? Marty pushed the thought aside. The tomorrows would have to care for themselves. She couldn't face too far into the future right now. She was sure if she let her mind focus on the weeks and months ahead of her in this tiny cabin with a husband she had not chosen and a child who was not hers, she'd break under the weight of it all.

She finished her final task of the day just in time to begin supper preparations. Clark had said he should be home for the usual chore time. She thumbed through the recipes Ma had left. She'd fix biscuits and a vegetable stew, she decided, using some of the meat broth Ma had brought to flavor the stew. She went to work, discovering that she had overlooked stoking the fire again.

"Dad-burn it. Will I never learn?" she fretted as she set to work to rebuild it. Missie, clutching her doll, watched it all with wide eyes.

"Da'-bu'n it," Marty heard the little girl murmur and couldn't help but feel a bit sheepish. She took a deep breath to calm herself, and the vegetables were simmering nicely when the team pulled up outside. Clark unhitched the wagon near the house to make it easier to unload the supplies, then went on to the barn with the horses.

Marty continued her supper preparations. This time, thanks to Ma Graham, the biscuits looked far more promising.

She noticed that Clark looked weary when he came in from his chores. He gave Missie a warm hug before he sat down at the table, but Marty thought his shoulders seemed to droop a bit. Was shopping really that hard on a man, or had she made the list too long and spent all his money? Marty mulled it over from her place at the table, but there didn't seem to be an answer, so she concentrated on cooling Missie's stew.

"'Fraid the totin' in of all of the supplies will sort of mess up yer well-ordered house fer the moment." Clark's voice interrupted her thoughts.

"Thet's okay," Marty responded. "We'll git them in their proper place soon enough."

"A lot of the stock supplies will go up in the loft over the kitchen," Clark went on. "Ya reach it by a ladder on the outside of the house."

Marty felt her eyes widen. "I didn't know there'd be a loft up there," she told him.

"It's nigh empty right now, so there wasn't much use in yer knowin'. We stock it up in the fall so's we won't run out of sech things as flour an' salt come the winter storms. I'll carry the stock supplies direct up so's I won't have to clutter yer house with 'em. The smaller things, though, I'll have to bring in here so's ya can put 'em all away in the place where ya want 'em. Do ya be wantin' 'em in the kitchen or in the shed?"

Marty knew it would be handier in the kitchen, yet if they were in the shed, there wouldn't be such a clutter until she got them put away. She decided on the shed, and they hurried through their supper in order to get at the task.

After they had finished eating, Clark pulled from his pocket a small bag of sweets and offered one to Missie. Then he gave the sack to Marty, telling her to help herself and then tuck it away in the cupboard for future treats. Missie sucked in noisy enjoyment, declaring it "num" and "Pa's yummy."

Marty washed the dishes, and Clark brought the supplies into the shed as they had agreed.

As she filled cans and crocks, Marty felt heady with the bounty of it all. She could hear Clark as he labored under the heavy bags, climbing again and again up the ladder to the kitchen loft.

At last it was all done. The cupboards were bulging. Imagine if she and Clem could have stocked up like that. Wouldn't it have been like Christmas and picnics and birthdays all wrapped up in one? She sighed and wiped away an unexpected tear.

Marty was tucking Missie in for the night, wondering if Clark was going to come hear the little girl's prayers as he usually did, when she heard him struggling with a rather heavy load. Marty's curiosity led her back to the kitchen to investigate. Clark, hammer in hand, was removing a crate enclosing some large object. She stood watching silently from the door while Clark's tool unmasked the contents. Her breath caught in her throat, for there, shining with metal and polished wood, stood the most wondrous sewing machine she had ever seen.

Clark did not look her way but began speaking, his voice sounding as weary as his shoulders had looked. But he seemed to feel that some kind of explanation was in order.

"I ordered it some months back as a surprise fer my Ellen. She liked to sew an' was al'ays makin' somethin' fancy like. It was to be fer her birthday. She would have been twenty-one—tomorrow." Clark looked up then. "I'd be proud if ya'd consider it yourn now. I'm sure ya can make use of it. I'll move it into yer room under the window iffen it pleases ya."

Marty swallowed back a sob. He was giving her this beautiful machine. She had always dreamed of having a machine of her own, but never had she dared to hope for one so grand. She didn't know what to say, yet she felt she must say something.

"Thank ya," she finally was able to murmur. "Thank ya. Thet . . . thet'll be fine, jest fine."

Only then did she realize that this tall man before her was fighting for control. His lips trembled and as he turned away, she was sure she saw tears in his eyes. Marty brushed by him and went out into the coolness of the night. She had to think, to sort things out. He had ordered the machine for his Ellen, and he was weeping. *He must be suffering, too,* she thought, stunned by the realization. The weary sag of his shoulders, the quivering lips, the tear-filled eyes. *He . . . he must understand something of how I'm feeling.* Somehow she had never thought of him as carrying such deep sorrow. Hot tears washed down Marty's cheeks.

Oh, Clem, her heart cried. *Why do sech things, sech cruel things, happen to people? Why? Why?*

But Marty knew there was no easy answer. This was the first time Clark had mentioned his wife. Marty hadn't even known her name. Indeed, she had been so wrapped up in her own grief she had not even wondered much about the woman who had been Clark's wife, Missie's mama, and the keeper of this house. Now her mind was awake to it. The rose by the door, the bright cheery curtains, Missie's lovingly sewn garments that she was too quickly outgrowing, the many colorful rugs on the floor. Everything—everything in this little home spoke of this woman. Marty felt like an intruder. What had she been like, this Ellen? Had she ever boiled the coffee over or made a flop of the biscuits? No, Marty was sure she hadn't. But she had been so young—only twenty-one tomorrow—and she was already gone. True, Marty was even younger—nineteen, in fact—but still, twenty-one seemed so young to die. And why did she die? Marty didn't know. There were so many things she didn't know, but a few things were becoming clear to her. There had been a woman in this house who loved it and made it a home, who gave birth to a baby daughter whom she cherished, a young woman who shared days and nights with her husband. Then he had lost her, and his loss had left him in grief and pain—like she was experiencing over losing her Clem. She had assumed she was the only one who bore that kind of sorrow, but it wasn't so.

It's a mean world, she mused as she turned her face upward. "It's mean an' wicked an' cruel," she said out loud as she gazed upward.

The stars blinked down at her from a clear sky.

"It's mean," she whispered, "but it's beautiful." What was it Ma Graham had said? *"Time,"* she'd said, *"it is time that's the healer—time an' God."* Marty supposed she meant Clark's God.

"Iffen we can carry on one day at a time, the day will come when it gets easier an' easier, an' one day we'll surprise ourselves by even bein' able to laugh an' love agin." That's what Ma had said.

It seemed so far away to Marty, but somehow she had confidence that Ma Graham should know.

Marty turned back to the house. It was cool in the evening now, and she realized she was shivering. When she entered the kitchen she found that all traces of the machine and the crate had been removed.

On the kitchen table was a large package wrapped with brown paper and tied with store twine. Clark motioned toward it.

"I'm not sure what might be in there," he said. "I asked Missus McDonald at the store to make up whatever a woman be needin' to pass the winter. She sent this. I hope it passes."

Marty took a deep breath. Just what did he mean? She wasn't sure.

"Would ya like me to be movin' it in on yer bed so's ya can be a sortin' through it?"

Without waiting for her answer, which may have taken half the night, she felt so tongue-tied, he carried it through to her room and placed it on her bed. He turned to leave.

"It's been a long day," he said quietly. "I think I'll be endin' it now," and he was gone.

Marty's fingers fumbled as she lit the lamp. Then she hurried to untie the string. Remembering the scissors in the sewing basket, she hurried to get them to speed up the process. She could hardly wait, but as the brown paper fell away she was totally unprepared for what she found.

There was material for undergarments and nighties and enough lengths for three dresses. One piece was warm and soft looking in a pale blue-gray; already her mind was picturing how it would look done up. It would be her company and visiting dress. It was beautiful. She explored further and found a pattern for a bonnet and two pieces of material. One lightweight and one heavier for the colder weather.

There was lace for trimming, and long warm stockings, and even a pair of shoes, warm and high for the winter, and a shawl for the cool days and evenings, and on the bottom, of all things, a long coat. She was sure no one else in the whole West would have clothing to equal hers. Her cheeks were warm and her hands trembled. Then with a shocked appeal to her senses, she pulled herself upright.

"Ya little fool," she muttered. "Ya can't be takin' all this. Do ya know thet iffen ya did, ya'd be beholden to thet man fer years to come?"

Resentment filled Marty. She wanted the things, the lovely things, but oh, she couldn't possibly accept them. What could she do? She would not humble herself and be beholden to this man. She would not be a beggar in his home. Tears scalded her cheeks. Oh, what could she do? What could she do?

"We are not fancy, but we try an' be proper" came back again to haunt her.

Could it be that he was embarrassed by her shabbiness? Yes, she decided, it could well be. Again her chin came up.

Okay, she determined, she'd take it—all of it. She would not be an embarrassment to any man. She would sew up the clothes in a way that would be the envy of every woman around. After all, she could sew. Clark need not feel shame because of her.

But the knowledge of what she knew—or thought she knew—drained much of the pleasure from the prospect of the new clothes.

In his lean-to bedroom, Clark stretched long, tired legs under the blankets. It had been a hard day for him, fraught with difficult memories.

It used to be such fun to bring home the winter supplies to Ellen. She had made such a fuss over them. Why, if she'd been there today she would have had Missie sharing in the game and half wild with excitement. Well, he certainly couldn't fault Marty, only five days a widow. He couldn't expect her to be overly carried away about salt and flour at this point. She must be in deep hurt, in awful grieving. He wished he could be of some help to her, but how? His own pain was still too sharp. It took time, he knew, to get over a loss like that, and he hadn't had enough time yet. The thought of wanting another woman had never entered his head since he'd lost Ellen. If it weren't for Missie, this one wouldn't be here now; but Missie needed her even if he didn't, and one could hardly take that out on the poor girl.

At first he had resented her here, he supposed—cleaning Ellen's cupboards, working at her stove—but no, that wasn't fair, either. After all, she hadn't chosen to be here. He'd just have to try harder to be decent and to understand her sorrow. He didn't want Missie in an atmosphere of gloom all the time. No, he'd have to try to shake the feeling, and in time maybe Marty could, too, so that the house would be a fit place for a little girl to grow and learn. *It's going to be harder for Marty,* he thought, *as she is all alone.* She didn't have a Missie, or a farm, or anything really. He hoped Mrs. McDonald had selected the right items for Marty. She really was going to need warmer things for the winter ahead.

The idea that he was doing anything special for her in getting her the things she needed did not enter his thinking. He was simply providing what was needed for those under his roof, a thing he had been taught was the responsibility of the man of the house when he was but a young'un tramping around, trying to keep up with the long strides of his own pa.

Nine

The Lord's Day

Sunday morning dawned bright and warm with only enough clouds in the sky to make an appealing landscape. At breakfast, hoping she wasn't too obvious, Marty asked Clark if he was through at Jedd's or if he'd be going back for the day. Clark looked at her with surprise.

"Jedd has him a bit more to finish off," he said, "an' I wouldn't be none surprised iffen he'd work at it today. Me, though, I al'ays take a rest on the Lord's Day. I know it don't seem much like the Lord's Day with no meetin', but I try an' hold it as sech the best I can."

Now it was Marty's turn for surprise. She would have known better if she had given it some thought, but in her eagerness for Clark to be away from the house, she hadn't considered it at all.

"'Course," she whispered, avoiding his eyes. "I'd plumb fergot what day it be."

Clark let this pass without further comment. After a moment or two, he said, "I been thinkin' as how me an' Missie might jest pack us a lunch an' spend the day in the woods. 'Pears like it may be the last chance fer a while. The air is gettin' cooler an' there's a feelin' in the air thet winter may be a mite anxious to be a comin'. We kinda enjoy jest spendin' the day lazyin' an' lookin' fer the last wild flowers an' smart-lookin' leaves an' all. Would thet suit yer plans?"

She almost stuttered. "Sure . . . sure . . . fine. I'll fix yer lunch right after breakfast."

"Good!"

It was settled, then. Clark and his little Missie would spend the day enjoying the outdoors and each other, and she, Marty, would have the day to herself. The thought both excited and frightened her. She wasn't too sure how she would do with no little girl around to help keep her thoughts from dwelling on her loss.

Clark went out into the shed and returned with a strange contraption that appeared to be some sort of carrier to be placed on his back.

"Fer Missie," he answered her unspoken question as she gazed at it. "I had to rig this up when I needed to take her to the fields an' a chorin' with me. She's even had her naps in it as I tramped along." He smiled faintly. "Little tyke's gotten right heavy at times, too, fer sech a tiny mite. Reckon I'd better take it along today fer when she tires of walkin'."

Marty realized she was giving them far more lunch than they needed, but the fresh air and the walk through the hills was bound to give them a hearty appetite.

Missie was beside herself with excitement and called good-bye over and over to Marty as they left. Ole Bob joined them at the door, and Marty watched the trio disappear behind the barn. As she turned back to clear the table and do up the dishes, she remembered that today would have been Ellen's birthday. Maybe their walk would include a visit to her gravesite. Marty somehow believed that it would.

She hurried through the small tasks of the morning and then fairly bolted to her bedroom and the waiting material and shiny new machine. She wasn't sure if she was breaking Clark's Sabbath with her sewing or not. She hoped not, but she was not sure she could have restrained from doing so even if she had known. She did hope she would not offend Clark's God. She needed any help He was inclined to give her. She pushed the thoughts aside and let her mind be completely taken up with her task—almost. At times she nearly caught her breath with feelings that came from nowhere.

Wouldn't Clem be proud to see me in this?

This is Clem's favorite color.

And later she whispered, "Clem al'ays did poke fun at what he called 'women's frivols.'" She couldn't help a little smile, but soon it got caught on the lump in her throat.

No, it seemed there was just no getting around it. Clem was there to disquiet her thoughts, and his absence still made her throat ache. Stubbornly she did not give in to the temptation to throw herself on her bed and sob, but she worked on with set jaw and determined spirit.

In the afternoon she laid her sewing aside. She hadn't even stopped for anything to eat. She hadn't missed it, though, and her sewing had been going well. The machine worked like a dream, and she couldn't believe how much faster seams were turned out with its help. She decided, however, that her eyes could use a rest, after staring so long at the machine foot. And her legs and feet were tiring after pumping the treadle all this time.

She walked outside, stretching her arms toward the sky. It was a glorious fall day, and she almost envied Clark and Missie's romp through the crackling leaves. Slowly she walked around the yard. The rosebush had one single bloom—not as big or as pretty as the earlier ones, she was sure, but beautiful just for its being there. She went on to the garden. The vegetables, for the most part, had already been harvested. Only a few things remained to be taken to the root cellar. At the end of the garden was the hole she had dug to bury her biscuits. It had been redug by Ole Bob, who felt it was his duty to unearth them again. A few dirty hard lumps still lay near the hole—even Ole Bob had abandoned them. It no longer mattered as much, Marty thought as she gave one a kick with her well-worn shoe. Funny how quickly things can change.

She walked on, savoring the day. The fruit trees that Clark had told her of looked promising and healthy. Wouldn't it be grand to have your own apples? Maybe even next year, Clark had said. She stood by one of the trees, not sure if it was an apple tree or not, but should it be, she implored it to please, please have some apples next year. She then remembered that even if it did, she would be long gone for the East by then. She didn't bother to inform the apple tree of this, for fear that it would lose heart and not bear after all. She turned and left, not caring as deeply now.

On she walked, down the path to the stream just behind the smokehouse. She found a stone platform that had been built into the creek bed where a spring, cold from the rocky hillside, burst forth to join the waters below. The perfectly shaded spot cooled crocks of butter and cream in the icy cold water on hot summer days. Clark hadn't told her about this, but then, there had been no reason to, it not being needed this time of year. She paused a moment, watching the gurgling water ripple over the polished stones. There was something so fascinating about water, she told herself as she moved away, and this would be a choice place to be refreshed on a sultry summer day. But of course she wouldn't be here then, she reminded herself once again.

She went on to the corrals, reaching over the fence to give Dan, or was it Charlie, a rub on his strong neck. The cows lay in the shade of the tall poplars, placidly chewing their cuds while their calves of that year grew fat on meadow grass in the adjoining pasture. *This is a good farm,* Marty decided—just the kind Clem and she had dreamed of having.

Giving her head a quick shake, she started for the house, past the henhouse. She suddenly felt a real hunger for panfried chicken. She hadn't realized how long it had been since she had tasted any, and she remembered home and the rich aroma from her ma's kitchen. At that moment she was sure nothing else would taste so good. Preparing chicken was one thing she had watched her mother do. Whenever they were to have fried chicken, she would station herself by her ma's kitchen table and observe the whole procedure from start to finish. Her mother had never begun with a live bird, though. Marty had never chopped off a chicken's head before, but she was sure she could manage somehow.

She walked closer to the coop, eyeing the chickens as they squawked and scurried around while she tried to pick out a likely candidate. She wasn't sure if she should first catch the one she wanted and then take it to the axe, or if she should go to the woodshed for the axe and bring it to the chicken. She finally decided she would take the chicken to the axe, realizing that she would need a chopping block as well.

She entered the coop and picked out her victim, a cocky young rooster that looked like he would make good frying.

"Come here, you, come here," she coaxed, stretching out her hand, but she soon caught on to the fact that a chicken would not respond like a dog. In fact, chickens seemed to be completely something else. They flew and squawked and whipped up dirt and chicken droppings like a mad whirlwind whenever she got to within grabbing distance of them. Marty soon decided that if she was to have a chicken for supper, full pursuit was the only way to get one into the pan. She abandoned herself to an outright chase, grabbing at chicken legs and ending up with a faceful of scattered dirt and dirty feathers. Round and round they went. By now Marty had given up on the cocky young rooster and had decided to settle for anything she could get her hands on. Finally, after much running and grabbing that had her dress soiled, her hair flying, and her temper seething, she managed to grasp hold of a pair of legs. He was heavier than she had expected, and it took all her strength to hold him, since he was determined he wasn't going to be supper for anyone. Marty held tight, just as determined. She half dragged him from the coop and looked him over. This was big boy himself, she was sure, the granddaddy of the flock, the ruler of the place. So what, she reasoned. He'd make a great panful, and maybe the bird hated the thought of facing another winter, anyway.

Panting with exhaustion as she headed for the woodshed,

Marty nonetheless felt very pleased with herself to have accomplished her mission.

She stretched the squawking, flopping rooster across a chopping block, and as he quieted, she reached for the axe. The flopping resumed, and Marty had to drop the axe in order to use both hands on the fowl. Over and over the scene was repeated. Marty began to think it was a battle to see who would wear out first. Well, she wouldn't be the one to give up.

"Ya dad-blame bird—hold still," she hissed at him and tried again, getting in a wild swing at the rooster's head.

With a squawk and a flutter, the rooster wrenched free and was gone, flopping and complaining across the yard. Marty looked down at the chopping block and beheld in horror the two small pieces of beak that remained there.

"Serves ya right!" she blazed, kicking the pieces off the block into the dirt.

Still determined not to be beaten, she headed again for the coop, while one short-beaked rooster still flapped about the farm, screaming out his wrath to a dastardly world.

Marty marched resolutely to the coop and began all over again. After many minutes of chasing and gulping against the flying dust, she finally got what she was after. This fellow was more her size, and again she set out for the chopping block. Again things didn't go well there. She stretched him out and reached for the axe, dropped the axe and stretched him out, over and over again. Finally she got inspired, and taking the chicken with her, she headed for the house. Into her bedroom she went, bird firmly under her arm, and took from a drawer the neatly wound roll of store string. Back at the woodshed, she sat down on a block with the chicken in her lap and securely tied the legs together. Then she carried him outside and tied the other end of the string to a small tree. Still holding the chicken, she tied another piece of string to his neck. She tied the second string to another small tree. She brought the chopping block from the woodshed and placed it in the proper spot beneath the chicken's outstretched neck.

"There now," she said with some satisfaction and, taking careful aim, she shut her eyes and chopped hard.

It worked—but Marty was totally unprepared for the next event. A wildly flopping chicken—with no head—covered her unmercifully with spattered blood.

"Stop thet! Stop thet!" she screamed. "Yer s'pose to be dead, ya—ya dumb headless thing."

She took another swing with the axe, relieving the chicken of one wing. Still it flopped, and Marty backed up against the shed as she tried to shield her face from the awful onslaught. Finally the chicken lay still, with only an occasional tremor. Marty took her hands from her face.

"Ya dad-blame bird," she stormed and wondered briefly if she dared pick it up.

She looked down at her dirty, bloodstained dress. What a mess, and all for a chicken supper.

Out in the barnyard an indignant short-beaked rooster tried to crow as Marty picked up the sorry mess of blood and feathers and headed for the house.

All of those feathers had to come off, and then came the even more disgusting job of cleaning out the innards.

Somehow she got through it all, and after she had washed the meat in fresh well water and seasoned it, she put it in the frypan with savory butter. She decided she'd best get cleaned up before Clark and Missie returned. A bath seemed to be the simplest and quickest way to care for the matter, so Marty hauled a basin into her room and filled it with warm water. When she was clean again, she took the dreadfully dirty dress and put it to soak in the bath water. She'd deal with that tomorrow, she promised herself as she carried the whole mess outside and placed it on a wash table beside the cabin.

Feeling refreshed and more herself after her bath, Marty resumed her preparations for supper. When Clark and Missie arrived, tired but happy from their day together, they were greeted by the smell of frying chicken. Clark's face showed no surprise, and their exchanges were matter-of-fact as Marty welcomed the two in for supper.

Indeed, Clark could hardly contain his surprise during the meal and had been on the verge of asking Marty if she'd had company that day, so sure was he that she must have had help to accomplish what a chicken for supper would require. But he'd thought better of such a question. After supper, on the way to the barn, he saw the soiled dress in the red-stained water and the mess by the woodshed. The chopping block was still where Marty had left it, though Ole Bob had already carted off the chicken's head. The store twine was there, too, still attached to the small trees.

As he passed the coop he could tell there had been some general upheaval there as well. It looked like the chickens had flopped in circles for hours—feathers and dirt were everywhere, including in the overturned feeding troughs and watering pans.

What really topped all was the old rooster angrily perched

on the corral fence with his ridiculously short beak, clacking away to beat the band.

"Well, I never," muttered Clark, shaking his head in amazement.

He couldn't help but smile at the sight of that rooster. Tomorrow he'd do something about him. Tonight he was thankful for Marty's meal of fried chicken.

Ten

Neighborly Hog Killin'

Marty mentally braced herself for the new week, hoping with all her heart that it would be packed full of activity.

Monday morning, Clark brought in the big rooster, beheaded and plucked. He advised Marty to boil rather than try to fry the patriarch of the flock, and Marty didn't mind taking his advice. After cleaning the bird and putting him on to cook in her largest pot, Marty set to work washing up all the clothing she could find that needed washing. Her back ached from the scrub board, and she was glad to spend the rest of the day at her sewing. She was surprised at how easy it was to care for Missie. The little one was quite content with a big wooden spoon and a bowl to stir up pretend meals for her dolly. Marty decided she'd make some new doll clothes when she had time.

The rest of the week was packed full, too. She went with Clark to Ben Graham's for the killing of the hogs. Todd Stern and his near-grown son, Jason, were there, too, and Marty recognized them as the kind neighbors who had brought Clem's body back and supplied his burying place. The pain was there, sharp and hurting again, but she made a real effort to push it from her. She was glad to be with Ma Graham. She felt able to draw so much strength, wisdom, and advice from the older woman.

As the day went on, Marty could not help but notice the looks that were exchanged between young Jason and Ma's Sally Anne. If she didn't miss her guess, something was brewing there.

She had little time to ponder on it, however, for the cutting and preparing of the meat was a big job. After the menfolk had done the killing and the scraping and had quartered the animals, the women were hard pressed to keep up with them.

The job that Marty found hardest to stomach was the emptying and preparing of the casings for the sausage meat. Floods of nausea swept over her, and several times she had to fight for control. When they were finally done, Marty went to the outhouse and lost all her dinner. She was glad to be rid of it and went back to work feeling some better.

The men looked after preparation of the salt brine for curing the bacon and hams and readied the smokehouse for the process. The women ground and seasoned the sausage meat and had the slow, rather boring task of stuffing the casings and tying them into proper lengths. It helped to be able to chat as they worked; still the job seemed a tedious one. On the second and third days, Hildi Stern came with her menfolk, and the extra hands aided much in getting the job done.

Lard had to be chopped up and rendered, some kept for cooking and frying and some put aside to be used in the making of soap.

By the end of each day, those involved were tired and aching.

Marty noticed that Ma tried to assign her the less-demanding tasks, but Marty would have none of it, wanting to do her full share.

At the end of the third day, the meat was divided up and things were cleaned up and put away for the next year's killing. Ma's Sally Anne put on the coffee for them all. They needed to renew their strength for the work that waited at home at day's end. Marty noticed Jason look in Sally's direction and saw her face flush beneath it. She couldn't fault Jason. Sally Anne was a very pretty seventeen-year-old, and just as sweet as she was pretty, Marty thought. Was Jason good enough for her? Marty hoped so. She knew nothing of the boy to make her think otherwise. He looked strong, and he certainly had been carrying his share of the work the last few days. He seemed mannerly enough. Yes, she summed it up—maybe he'd be all right. Anyway, it looked like he'd have to be, the way they were mooning over each other.

She remembered again how it had been when she had first met Clem—when his eyes turned toward her, she could feel him watching even when she wasn't looking directly at him, and her cheeks would flush in her excitement. She had known right away that she would love him, and she guessed he had known it, too. His very presence had sent fireworks through her. She had felt she couldn't wait to see him again, but she could hardly bear it when she did. She had thought she'd ex-plode with the intensity of it, but that's what love was like. Wild and possessing, making one nearly burst with excitement and desire—being both sweet and painful at the same time. Yes, that's how love was.

Clark was excusing himself from the table and Marty got

up, too. She said the necessary thank-yous and good-byes to Ma Graham and eyed the crocks of lard she was to take home for making soap.

"No use us both gittin' ourselves in a mess makin' soap," Ma Graham said. "Marty, why don't ya leave them crocks here an' come over in the mornin' an' we'll do it all up together like?"

Bless ya, Ma Graham, Marty's heart cried. *Ya know very well I'd be downright lost on my own tryin' to make soap fer the first time.*

She looked at Clark for his reaction.

"Sounds like a good plan ta me," Clark responded.

"Thank ya, Ma," Marty said with feeling. "I'll be over in the mornin' jest as soon as I can."

Thank-you seemed very inadequate for the gratitude she felt.

Eleven

Togetherness

Marty kept her word and hurried through the morning household chores so she could do her rightful share of the work at Ma's. As she went for Missie's coat and bonnet, Clark spoke up.

"I've nothin' pressin' to take my time today. Thought I'd be doin' the caulkin' here in the kitchen. Why don'cha jest leave Missie to home with me, an' then ya won't need to worry ya none 'bout her gittin' underfoot around those hot pots."

Marty nodded her appreciation and agreement and hurried to the team and wagon that Clark had waiting.

It was cooler today. In fact, there was almost a chill to the air. Maybe winter would soon be coming. Marty did not look forward to those long days and even longer evenings that stretched out before her.

The soapmaking was a demanding, hot job, and Marty was glad when they were finished. The soap mixture was placed in pans, ready to be cut into bars after it had cooled.

The two women sat down for a much-needed cup of coffee

and one of Ma's slices of johnnycake. There did not seem to be much chance for confidential talking at Ma's place. What with eleven children crowding every corner of the small house, there was seldom an opportunity to be alone. But Ma talked freely, ignoring the coming and going.

She told Marty that her first husband, Thornton Perkins, had been the owner of a small store in town, and when he had come to an early death, he had left her with the business and three small children to provide for. When Ben Graham came along with good farmland and the need for a woman, he appeared to be the answer to prayer, even though he had four small ones of his own tagging along behind him. So they had joined forces, the young widow with three and the widower with four. To that union had been born six more children. One they had lost as a baby and one at the age of seven. The seven-year-old had been one of Ma's, but Ben, too, had felt the loss deeply. Now the children numbered eleven, and every one of them was special.

Sally Anne and Laura were both seventeen, only two months apart, with Ben's Laura being the older. Next came Ben's Thomas, then Ma's Nellie. Ma's Ben had been next, and Ma supposed one of the reasons Ben had become so attached to this boy was that they both bore the same name. Ben's twins were next in line, Lem and Claude. They were named after their two grandfathers. The younger children Marty still didn't have sorted out by name. There was a Faith and a Clint, she knew, and she believed she had heard the little one called Lou.

It was the two older girls that most interested Marty. Sally Anne was one of the prettiest young things Marty had ever seen, and the girl seemed to simply adore her stepsister Laura. Laura, though capable and efficient, was plain and probably knew it, for she seemed to always be trying to outdo Sally Anne. *Why does she do it?* Marty puzzled. *Can't she see that Sally Anne practically worships her? Laura has no earthly reason to lord it over her.* In watching more closely, she decided that Laura was unaware of what she was doing, probably driven by a deep feeling of being inferior to her pretty sister.

She doesn't need to feel thet way, Marty reasoned silently. *She has so much to offer jest the way she be.*

She supposed there was nothing she could do about it. However, she promised herself that she'd try to be especially nice to Laura and maybe help her realize she was a worthwhile person.

It was getting to be late afternoon, and Marty knew she must be on her way.

She thanked Ma sincerely for all her help with the soap. Now she felt confident that she'd be able to do it on her own the next time. She told Ma that if she could spare the time, she'd sure appreciate another visit from her before the snow shut them in. Ma promised to try and, giving Marty a hearty hug, sent her on her way.

When Marty reached home, Clark came out of the cabin to take over the team, and he brought Missie with him for the brief trip to the barn. As Marty entered the kitchen, she saw that all of the old crumbled chinking had been replaced with new and was rapidly turning to the proper attractive white. Now she wouldn't be sweeping up pieces of it each time she cleaned the kitchen floor. Though she was still embarrassed about her inadvertent error, she was glad the chinking was fixed and noted with appreciation that Clark had even cleaned up any mess he had made in completing the job.

Marty was tired as she began supper preparations, and she knew she would be very glad when it was time to go to bed. Tomorrow was Saturday, so she must first make a list for Clark, since he would want to leave for town early the next morning.

Twelve

Finishin' My Sewin'

Clark did leave early for town the next day, and Marty sighed with relief as she watched him disappear with the wagon and team. She still felt him to be a stranger to avoid whenever she could; though, without realizing it, some of her emotional turmoil was seeping away simply because, deep down, she realized her anger toward Clark was unfounded. They were victims of circumstances, both of them, forced to share the same house. Notwithstanding, Marty still was much relieved when his duties took him elsewhere.

The supply list hadn't been as long this time, but Clark had asked her to check through Missie's clothing to see what the child would be needing for the winter. Marty did this and carefully added some items to the list. Then Clark stood Missie on a chair and traced a pattern of her small foot so he could bring back shoes for her growing feet.

Marty busied herself with her morning routine. She still felt tired from the day of soapmaking. In fact, she wondered if the emotionally driven hard work of cleaning, cooking, and sewing during the preceding days was not taking its toll. She felt drained and even slightly dizzy as she finished up the dishes. For the sake of the little one she was carrying, she must hold herself in check and not pour all her energy into frenzied activity. She had lost her Clem. Now, more than ever, she wanted his baby.

Marty decided she would make this day an easier one. She did household chores for the day, sweeping and tidying each small room. Her bedroom had become quite crowded with her bed, Missie's crib, two chests, her trunk, the sewing basket, and the new machine. She wouldn't complain, she thought, as she looked at the beautiful shining thing. There really was more room for it in the sitting room, but she was sure that for Clark to have to see it continually would be a hurtful reminder. No, she'd be glad to spare him that much, and she ran a loving hand over the polished wood and gleaming metal.

"Today, Missie," she spoke to the child, "I'm gonna finish my sewin'."

She moved across to the garments she had already made and fingered them with pride. There hung the newly made bonnets, one of light material, a little more dressy, the other of warm, sturdy cloth for the cold days ahead. There were the underclothes, some trimmed with bits of lace. She had never had such feminine things before. She almost hated to wear them and take away their fresh newness. Two nighties lay folded in the drawer. She had put extra tucks and stitching on them, and one had some dainty blue trim. Two dresses hung completed. They were not fancy, but they were neat and attractive, and Marty felt confident that Clark would deem them "proper."

Beside her chest stood the new shoes, still black and shiny.

She had not as yet worn them. As long as she could, she would wear her old ones and keep the new ones to admire. Her new coat and shawl, so very new and beautiful, hung on pegs behind the door.

Marty sighed. She had only the blue-gray material left to make up. She had saved it until last because it was to be special. She let the beautiful material lay against her hand, then lifted one corner to her cheek.

"Missie," she half whispered, "I'm gonna make me a dress. Ya jest wait until you see it. It's gonna be so grand, an' maybe— maybe when I be all through, there be enough material left to make ya somethin', too."

Suddenly that was important to Marty. She wanted, with all her heart, to share this bit of happiness with someone, and Missie seemed the likely one to share it with.

"Maybe I'll even have enough for a dolly dress," Marty added as Missie patted the material and proclaimed it "pwetty." Marty went to work. Missie played well on the rug by the bed, and the sewing machine hummed along. When Missie became restless, Marty was shocked to find the clock said ten past one.

"Oh dear!" Marty exclaimed, picking up the child. "Missie, I'm plumb sorry. It be long past yer dinnertime. Ya must be awful hungry. I'll git ya somethin' right away."

They ate together and then Marty tucked Missie in for her nap. The child fell asleep listening to the steady whir of the machine.

The new dress took shape, and when she had carefully finished each tuck and seam, Marty held it up. It nearly took her breath away. She was sure she had never had one quite so pretty. She had added some width for her use now, but she would easily be able to take it in after her baby arrived. She couldn't resist trying on the dress and frankly admiring herself. She removed it reluctantly and carefully hung it with her other dresses, arranging each fold to hang just right.

Eagerly she set to work on the small garment for Missie. She decided to make a small blouse from the white material that was left over from her underthings, with a jumper for over it from the blue-gray wool. She had enough to do the same for the worn little doll.

The blouse was soon completed, and with great care Marty set to work on the tiny jumper. The tucks were fussed over to make sure they were just so, and each seam was sewn with utmost care. When Marty was finished she made small decorative stitches across the yoke with needle and thread.

Missie, who had long since awakened from her nap, kept demanding to see the "pwetty," and Marty's work would be interrupted while she showed her.

Suddenly Marty jumped from her chair as she heard Ole Bob welcoming Clark home.

"Dad-burn," she said, hastily laying her sewing aside and hurrying to the kitchen. "I haven't even thought me about supper."

The stove was cold to her touch. She had forgotten all day to replenish its fuel.

Clark had driven on down to the barn. The supplies would not take as many trips to carry this time, nor would they be as heavy to tote.

Marty rushed about the kitchen. She remembered an old secret of her ma's. If the menfolk come looking for their supper and you're caught off guard, quickly set the table. That will make them think supper is well on the way.

In a mad flurry, Marty hastened to throw on the plates and cutlery. Then she flushed at her foolishness. That wouldn't trick Clark. He had nearly an hour of choring ahead and wouldn't be looking for plates on yet. A stove with a fire in it might be a bit more convincing. When Clark came in, Marty was building the fire and wondering what she could have ready for supper in a very short time.

After depositing his armload of purchases, Clark went back out to do the chores, and Marty set to work in earnest preparing the supper.

When Clark returned from the barn, the meal was ready, simple though it was. Marty made no apology. After all, she told herself, it wasn't as though she had whiled away the whole day. Nevertheless, she promised herself not to let it happen again.

After the supper dishes had been cleared away, Clark brought out his purchases for little Missie. She was wild in her excitement, hugging the new shoes, jumping up and down about the new coat and bonnet, and running around in circles waving her new long stockings in the air. She exclaimed over the material to be sewn into little frocks, but Marty was sure the tiny child didn't really understand what it was all about. She returned to the shoes, pulled her bonnet on her head, back to front, and whirled another long stocking. Marty couldn't help but smile, understanding how the little girl felt.

Suddenly Missie turned and headed for the bedroom, a pair of the new stockings streaming out behind her. *She's going to put them in her chest,* Marty thought. In a moment the flying feet came running back and one of the tiny hands carried over her head the small jumper Marty had been working on. Marty watched as Missie pushed the garment onto Clark's lap, pointing at the fancy stitching and exclaiming, "Pwetty. Mine. Pwetty."

Clark carefully picked up the jumper in his big work-roughened hands. His eyes softened as he looked across at Marty. She held her breath. For a moment he did not speak but sat quietly stroking the small garment. His voice sounded a bit choked as he responded, "Yeah, Missie, very pretty," but it was to Marty that he spoke, not the excited child.

Clark had more surprises. For Missie he had a picture book. She had never seen such a wondrous thing before and spent the rest of the evening carefully turning the pages, exclaiming over and over her excitement at finding cows and pigs and bunnies in such an unlikely place. Clark had bought himself some books, too, for the long winter evenings ahead. This was the first time Marty was aware that Clark was a reader. She then remembered the shelf in the sitting room with a number of interesting-looking books on it. No doubt some of them had been favorites of Missie's mama. Maybe she herself would have time of a winter evening to read one or more of them.

Clark had a package for her, as well, that would help pass the months ahead. It contained wool and knitting needles and pieces of material for quilt piecing, and he told her he had a sack of raw wool that he had stored until such time as it was needed.

Marty was very thankful. She loved to knit, and though she had never quilted before, she was anxious to try her hand at it.

Missie was too excited to go to bed, but with a firmness that surprised Marty, Clark informed her that she'd had enough excitement for one night and all her things would be there in the morning. After Marty washed the child up and got her ready for bed, Clark tucked her in and heard her short prayer. Marty carefully folded the new things and picked up the pieces of material. *This will fill up a few more days,* she thought with relief. If only she could keep herself busy, perhaps she wouldn't feel so lonely and bereft. She placed everything in Missie's chest for the night, planning to go to work on sewing the little garments the next day.

Oh no, she suddenly remembered. *Tomorrow be another Lord's Day!*

She couldn't expect Clark and Missie to tramp off into the outdoors two Sundays in a row, especially when it was getting a bit chilly.

"Dad-burn!" she exclaimed softly.

How in the world would she be able to suffer through the long, miserable day anyway? Maybe she should wrap up well and take to the woods herself. Well, no use fretting about it now. She had a small amount of work to do yet on the jumper, and then she'd take her tired self off to bed. It seemed a usual thing these days for her to feel weary.

Thirteen

Ellen

Sunday was a cool day with a wind blowing from the west. After their morning reading and prayer, Marty's mind kept puzzling over the Scripture passage. "'The Lord is my shepherd,'" she heard Clark read from the Psalms. *How could the Lord be a shepherd?* she wondered. She gradually was listening more closely, and she found herself wanting to ask Clark a question or to repeat some portion so she might ponder its meaning. But she could not bring herself to ask him.

Could this God Clark was reading about be a comfort to others as He had been to the writer?—David, Clark said his name was. Marty acknowledged that she knew very little about God, and sometimes she caught herself yearning to know more. Bible reading hadn't been a part of her upbringing. She wondered in a vague way if she had missed out on something rather important. On occasion Clark would add a few words of his own as a background or setting to the Scripture for that day, telling a bit about the author and his troubled life at the time of his writing.

Marty knew that the explanation was intended for her, but she didn't resent it. Indeed, she was pleased with whatever added to her understanding.

During the morning prayer time, Marty found herself wondering if she dared to approach Clark's God in the direct way that Clark himself did. She felt a longing to do so, but she held back.

When Clark said "amen," Marty's lips also formed the words.

Breakfast began after Missie declared her loud "'men," too.

What on earth are we gonna do with this long day in front of us? Marty wondered silently. She knew that on this Lord's Day she should not sew. She had made that blunder once, but to repeat it would be tempting God's anger to fall upon her, and she couldn't risk that. If He could spare any help at all for her, she desperately needed it.

Clark interrupted her thoughts. "On the way to town yesterday, I stopped me at the Grahams' to see if there be anythin' thet I might be gettin' them in town. Ma asked thet we come fer a visit an' dinner today. Who knows how many nice Sundays we be a havin' afore winter sets in? I said I'd check with ya on it."

Bless ya, Ma, thought Marty. *Oh, bless ya!*

Out loud she quite calmly said, "I'd be likin' thet," and it was settled.

She hurried with the morning dishes, and while Clark went to get the team, she quickly got Missie and herself ready to go.

She dressed Missie in the new blouse and jumper with a pair of the new stockings and the little black shoes. She brushed out Missie's curls until they were light and fluffy. The child truly did look a picture as she twirled and pirouetted, admiring herself and clapping her little hands with excitement.

Marty then turned to her own apparel. She took the new blue-gray dress from the hanger and held it up to herself. It should have been for Clem, and somehow she just couldn't bring herself to put it on. If Clark failed to notice it, she would be disappointed, and if by some strange chance his eyes showed admiration, that would hurt even more. She didn't want admiration from him or any other man. She could still clearly see Clem's love-filled eyes as he pulled her to him. She smothered the sob in the folds of the dress and put it back on its hanger. She chose the plainer navy dress with the bit of lace trim at the throat and sleeves. Surely this one would be quite acceptable, even proper, for Sunday dinner with the neighbors.

She dressed in the new undergarments and long stockings, put on the new shoes, and slipped the dress over her head. She'd wear the lighter bonnet and her new shawl. It wasn't cold enough to be needing the heavy coat.

Carefully she brushed out her curly hair and then decided to pin it up fashionably. She had been dreadfully neglectful of it lately, she knew. It took her several minutes for her to arrange it appropriately. She was peering critically at herself in the small mirror on the wall when she heard Clark call from the door asking if they were ready.

Missie burst from the room to meet her pa and was informed that she looked like a "real little lady an' your pa is right proud of you."

Marty followed, avoiding Clark's eyes. She didn't want to read anything there, whether real or imagined. She noticed as he helped her up to the seat of the wagon that he had changed from his work clothes and looked rather fine himself. As they traveled to the Grahams', she gave her full attention to the young Missie and the lovely crisp fall day.

Marty helped Ma Graham and the girls get the dinner on. In contrast to the first time she found herself in the Graham home, Marty now was able to concentrate, and she found Ma to be a very good cook, a fact that was no surprise to her after all the recipes she had provided. Following dinner, the men left for the sunny side of the porch for some man talk.

Young Jason Stern put in an appearance, much to the blushing of Sally Anne. The two went for a walk, always staying properly in full sight of the house.

The two women made quick work of the dishes, and then Ma and Marty sat down for their own chat. It felt so good just to sit and talk with Ma. Marty didn't mind the unusual idleness half so much with such pleasant company. After discussing general women's topics, Marty took advantage of the fact that the rest were outdoors and the two young ones down for a nap to raise a question.

"Ma," she ventured, "could ya tell me 'bout Ellen? Seems thet I should be knowin' somethin' 'bout her, since I be takin' over her house an' her baby."

Marty made no reference to "her man," and if Ma noticed, she made no sign of it. Marty told Ma about the sewing machine and Clark's reaction to it.

Ma sighed deeply and looked off into space for a moment. When she spoke, her voice was a mite shaky. "Don't hardly know what words to be a tellin' it with," Ma said. "Ellen was young an' right pretty, too. Darker than you, she be, an' taller, too. She was a merry and chattery sort. Loved everythin' an' everybody, seemed to me. She adored Clark, an' he 'peared to think her somethin' pretty special, too." Ma paused and looked into Marty's face, probably wondering how she was responding to this sensitive topic. Nodding thoughtfully, she continued her narrative.

"When Missie was born, ya should have see'd the two of 'em." Ma shook her head and smiled gently. "Never see'd two people so excited—like a couple of kids, they were. I delivered Missie. Fact is, I've delivered most babies here 'bouts, but never did I see anyone else git quite thet excited over a newborn, welcome as they normally be.

"Well, Ellen, she was soon up an' about an' fussin' over thet new baby. She thought she was jest beautiful, an' Missie be right pretty, too. Anyway, the months went by. Clark an' Ellen was a doin' real good. Clark's a hard worker, an' thet's what farmin' is all about. Ya git what yer willin' to pay fer in sweat an' achin' back. Well, things was goin' real good when one day last August Clark came ridin' into the yard. He was real agitated like, an' I knew thet somethin' was wrong. 'Ma,' he says, 'can ya come quick? Ellen is in awful pain.' Thet's what he says. I can hear him yet.

"So I went, yellin' to the girls what to do while I be gone. Ellen was in pain, all right, tossing an' rollin' on the bed, holdin' herself an' groanin'. She refused to cry out 'cause she didn't want Missie to hear her. So she jest bit her lip till she near had it a bleedin'.

"Wasn't much thet I could do but try to keep her face cooled. There was no doctor to go fer, an' we jest watched, in such pain ourselves over the fact thet we couldn't be doin' anythin' fer her. Clark was torn between stayin' with Ellen an' carin' fer Missie. I never been so sorry fer a man.

"Well, the night dragged by, an' finally 'bout four in the mornin' she stopped thrashin' so. I breathed a prayer of relief, but it wasn't to be fer long. She kept gettin' hotter an' hotter an' more an' more listless. I bathed her in cool water over an' over again, but it were no use."

Ma stopped for a moment, then took a deep breath and went on. "Thet evenin' we lost her, an' Clark—" She stopped again.

Ma brushed away a tear and stood up. "But thet be in the past, child, an' no use goin' over it all agin. Anyway, ya be there now to care fer Missie, an' thet's what Clark be a needin'. Was awful hard fer him to do all his fall work while totin' thet little one round on his back. I said I'd keep her on here, but I reckon Clark wanted her to know thet she be his an' somethin' special, not jest one of a brood. Besides, he never did want to be beholden to anybody. There was a childless couple in town who would have gladly took her, but Clark would have none of it. Said she needed her pa right then; that's what Clark said. Anyway, Clark's prayers seem to be gittin' answered, and Missie has you now an' a right good mama ya be a makin', too—sewin' thet sweet little dress an' all."

She patted Marty's arm. "Yer doin' jest fine, Marty. Jest fine."

Through the whole speech of Ma's, Marty had sat silent but listening with her heart as well as ears. The hearing of Clark's sorrow had opened afresh the pain of her own. She wanted to weep, but she sat dry eyed, feeling anew the sorrow of it all. It indeed had been a shock for her to hear that Clem was dead, but she hadn't had to sit by him for hours watching him suffer, not able to lift a hand to relieve him. She decided she probably'd had a mite easier suffering of the two.

Oh, Clem, her heart whispered. *Clem, I'm glad thet ya didn't have to bear pain like thet.*

She roused herself as Ma scrambled up, exclaiming that time had just flown and the menfolk would be looking for coffee.

Fourteen

Missie

The next morning at breakfast Clark informed Marty that the coming Thursday Missie would have her second birthday. Marty immediately felt concerned. She wasn't sure how Ellen would have celebrated the event. She didn't want to let Clark down, but how was she to know what the family chose to do about birthdays? She silently weighed the matter for the rest of the meal.

Clark must have sensed her mood because he finally inquired, "Somethin' be a troublin' ya?"

"No," Marty lied and remained silent for a few more minutes, then decided that would never do. If they had to share the same house, they'd just have to be frank and honest with each other, so she blurted out, "It's jest thet I don't know what ya would want planned fer Missie's birthday. Do ya have company? Have a party? Do somethin' different?" She shrugged. "I don't know."

"I see," Clark said, and she felt he really did understand. He got up and refilled their coffee cups.

Dad-blame, Marty scolded herself, *I missed thet second cup agin with my deep thinkin'.*

Clark didn't appear to be bothered by it. He sat back down and creamed his coffee, pushing his plate back and pulling his cup forward as though preparing for a lengthy stay.

By this time little Missie was getting restless and wanting down from her chair. Clark lifted her down and she ran to find her new book.

"Funny thing," Clark continued then, "but I don't rightly remember any fixed thing thet we be a doin' fer a birthday. Seems in lookin' back thet they were all a mite different somehow. Missie, now, she only had one afore, an' she was a bit young then to pay it much mind." He hesitated. "I think, though, thet it would be nice to be a havin' a cake fer her. I got a doodad in town last Saturday while I was there. I hope it pleases her. Jest a silly little thing, really, but it looks like it would tickle a little'un. I don't think thet we be needin' company's help in celebratin'. She'll enjoy it as much on her own with jest"—he paused slightly and finished quickly—"jest us."

Marty was relieved. That kind of a birthday celebration she felt she could manage. She sat quietly for a moment and finally raised her eyes to Clark's and said, "I been thinkin'. Seems thet I don't know much 'bout Missie, an' seems as though I should be a knowin' a sight more iffen I be goin' to raise her an' all. Ya know how young'uns be. They like to hear their folks tell of when they did this an' when they said thet, an' how cute an' clever they was, an' quick in their ways an' all. Someday soon Missie's goin' to be wantin' to hear sech things, an' I should be able to tell her. The only thing I really know 'bout her is her name."

Clark surprised her by laughing quietly. It was the first time she had heard him laugh. She liked it, but she couldn't figure out the reason for it. He soon explained.

"I be thinkin' thet ya don't really know even thet," he said with another chuckle. "Her real name be Melissa—Melissa Ann Davis."

"Thet's a pretty name," Marty said. "I don't be goin' by my real name, either. My real name be Martha, but I don't much like it. All my family an' friends called me Marty, 'cept my ma when she was upset. Then it was Martha, real loud like. Martha Lucinda—" She had nearly finished it with Claridge but caught herself in time. "But tell me 'bout Missie."

"Well, Missie be born on November third, two years ago, 'bout four o'clock in the mornin'."

Clark's face became very thoughtful as he reflected back. Marty remembered Ma telling of the great excitement that Missie's appearance had brought.

"She weren't much of a bundle," Clark went on. "Seemed to me she was rather red an' wrinkled an' had a good head of dark hair. She seemed to grow fast an' change a lot right from the start, an' afore ya knowed it she was a cooin' an' smilin'. By Christmastime she was most givin' the orders round here, it seemed. She was a good baby as babies go an' slept through the night by the time she was three months old. I thought I'd picked me a real winner. Then at five months she started to cut her teeth. She turned from a sweet, contented, smilin' darlin' into a real bearcat. Lucky fer us, it didn't last fer too long, though at the time it seemed forever. Anyway, she made it through. So did we, an' things quieted down agin.

"When she had her first birthday, she could already say some words. Seemed right bright for a little tyke, an' al'ays, from as far back as I can remember, she loved pretty things. Guess thet's why she took so to the little whatever it be thet ya sewed fer her.

"Started walkin' 'fore her first birthday an' was soon climbin' to match it. Boy, how she did git around! One day I found her on the corral fence, top rail, when she be jest a wee'un. Got up there an' couldn't git down. Hangin' on fer dear life, she was.

"She was gettin' to be a right good companion, too. A lot of company she was. Chattered all the time, an' more an' more there was gettin' to be some sense to it.

"One day she came in with a flower. Thrilled to pieces with it, she was. Picked it right off the rosebush. The thorns had pricked her tiny fingers an' they was a bleedin'. But she never paid them no mind at all, so determined she be to take the 'pretty' to her mama. Thet flower is pressed in her mama's Bible."

Clark stopped and sat looking at his coffee cup. Marty saw him swallow and his lips move as though he meant to go on, but no sound came.

"Ya don't need to tell me any more," she said quietly. "I know enough from this to be able to tell young Missie somethin' 'bout her young days."

She searched for something further to say and found that anything she could bring to mind seemed inadequate, but she stumbled on. "I know how painful it be—to remember, an' anyway when the day comes thet young Missie need hear the story of her mama—an' she should hear it, to be sure—but when thet day comes, it's her pa thet she should be hearin' it from."

Marty rose from the table then so that Clark need not worry about saying more. Slowly he finished his coffee, and she set to getting her water ready to wash the dishes.

The day was quite cool, but Clark announced that he planned

to see how much sod he could get turned on the land he was claiming for spring planting. Marty hoped the weather would hold, not just so that he could finish the plowing but also so that he would continue to be busy away from the house. She was getting more used to him, but she still felt awkward and at loose ends if he was in the house very long.

Sometimes the days went too slowly for Marty, but she was relieved when she could always find work with which to fill them. What with washing, cleaning, bread baking, and meal getting, she had to look for time in which to do Missie's sewing. Little garments did take shape under her capable hands, however, and Missie exclaimed in delight over each one of them.

Marty had a secret project in the works, as well. Missie's birthday had sent her mind scrambling over what she might be able to do for the little girl. She didn't have a cent to her name, even if she could have found a way to spend it. She then thought of the beautifully colored wool Clark had brought and the brand-new knitting needles. Each night she retired to her room as soon as her day's tasks were taken care of, and with Missie sleeping soundly in her crib, the knitting needles clicked hurriedly. She must work quickly to be done in time. When she finally crawled into bed each night, she was too tired to even lie for very long and ache for Clem. She thought of him, and her last wish of the night was that he could have been by her side, cuddling close in the big double bed. But even though her thoughts turned to him, her tired body demanded sleep, and she mostly felt too weary to even cry.

Thursday dawned cold and windy. Clark was still determined to carry on with his plowing. Marty hoped he would not take a chill by so doing. He paid no mind to her worries and went anyway. She wondered secretly if he wished to be away from the house as much as she wanted that.

After dinner was over and Missie had been put down for her nap, Marty went to work on the birthday cake. She felt much more confident now, having practiced with Ma's recipes. Carefully she watched her fire on this day. It would not do to have it too hot, nor to let it die out as she so often did.

She sighed with relief when she lifted Missie's cake from the oven. It appeared to be all that she had hoped for.

The wind was colder now and Marty found herself fussing about Clark. What in the world would she ever do if he took sick and needed nursing? *Dad-burn man! He shouldn't be taking such chances,* she scolded mentally. She'd keep the coffeepot on so whenever he decided to come in she'd have a hot cup waiting. She'd do almost anything, she figured, to keep him on his feet and walking. Why, if he went down sick, she wouldn't know where to start on the chores. She'd never even set foot in the barn, she realized. Some womenfolk had to do the milking all of the time, and for that matter, some did the slopping of the hogs, too. Clark hadn't even turned the feeding of the chickens over to her. Maybe he had expected it and she just hadn't done so. She had been so mixed up and confused when she came to this place that she hadn't given it a thought. Well, she'd ask. Maybe tomorrow at breakfast if the time seemed right. She was willing to do her rightful share.

She heard the team coming and cast a glance out the window.

"He be lookin' cold, all right," she murmured as she pushed the coffeepot forward on the stove.

When Clark came in, he stood for a few moments holding his big hands over the kitchen stove.

Marty poured his cup of coffee and went for some cream. She decided to also bring some muffins and honey in case he wanted a bite to go with the hot drink.

He watched her from the stove and said nothing until she had set it by his place at the table.

"Won't ya be a joinin' me?" he asked, then, "I hate to be a drinkin' coffee all alone."

Marty looked up in surprise but answered evenly, "Ya be the one thet be needin' it. Ya be chillin' yerself fer sure workin' out in thet wretched wind an' all. Lucky ya be iffen ya don't be a puttin' yerself down over it. Come, ya'd better be drinkin' this while it be hot."

It was a mild scolding, but something in it seemed to tickle Clark. He smiled to himself as he crossed to the table. She could hear his good-natured complaining. "Women—honestly, one would think a man was made o' sugar frostin' the way they can carry on." He looked at her directly and said, "I may be the one a needin' it, but I doubt thet a few minutes at the table an' off yer feet be a hurtin' ya much, either. You're doin' too much, I be a thinkin'." But his tone was kind.

"No," Marty said solemnly. "No, I don't do too much. I jest find thet workin' sure beats moanin', thet's all. But as ya say, a cup of coffee might be right good. I do declare, hearin' thet wind howl makes my blood chill, even though it be warm in here."

She poured herself a cup of coffee and joined him at the table.

After their coffee, Clark said he had come home early from the plowing because he thought a storm might be on the way and he wanted to have the rest of the garden things in the root cellar before it struck. So saying, he left the house.

Marty turned to Missie's now-cooled cake. She wanted it to

look special for the little girl, so she used all her ingenuity and ingredients available for that purpose. When she was finally done, she looked at it critically. It wasn't great, she decided, but it would have to do. She placed it in the cupboard behind closed doors to await the proper moment. She set to work on plans for a little something extra for supper. Missie's call from the bedroom interrupted her, and she went in for the little girl.

"Hi there, Missie. Come to Mama," she said.

She had said the words before and hadn't liked them, so she had not referred to herself as such since. But as she spoke them now, they didn't seem nearly so out of place.

She lifted the wee one from the bed, noticing as she did so that her own little one was demanding more room. She was glad she had put plenty of fullness in the new dresses she had made.

Missie ran to get her shoes, and Marty carried child and shoes to the kitchen, where she put them on. Already it was chilly in the bedroom. She did not look forward to the cold winter ahead. How glad she was not to be in the covered wagon. The very thought made her shiver.

She gave Missie a mug of milk and half a muffin and went back to preparing the evening meal.

Clark finished up the work in the garden and did the evening chores a bit earlier than usual. Marty sensed an excitement he had not shown before. She knew he must have dreaded the arrival of his little girl's birthday without Ellen there to share it, but she also knew he wanted to make the most of it for Missie's sake.

After they had finished their supper, Marty went to the cupboard for the cake. Missie's eyes opened wide in wonder, but she did not understand its meaning.

"Pwetty, pwetty!" she cried over and over.

"It's Missie's birthday cake," Clark explained. "Missie's havin' a birthday. Missie was one," he indicated with one upright finger, "now Missie be two." Another finger joined the first.

"See, Missie," her pa continued the explanation, "you're two years old. Here, let me help ya."

He took the small hand in his big one and helped Missie hold upright two fingers.

"See, Missie, ya be two years old."

"Two—old," Missie repeated.

"Thet's right," said Clark, sounding well pleased. "Two years old, an' now we'll have some of Missie's birthday cake."

Marty cut the cake and was surprised at how good it was. As she took a bite she thought of her first effort with the biscuits. Now, thankfully, with practice and Ma's recipes, she could turn out things that she need not be ashamed of. Three weeks had made quite a difference. And Clark asked for and received a second piece of cake.

When they had finished, Marty was about to wash the supper dishes, but Clark suggested they first see what Missie thought of the gift he had purchased.

Clark went out to the shed and returned with a small box; then lifting Missie out of her chair, he presented it to her.

"Fer Missie's birthday," Clark said.

Missie turned and looked at the cake, as though wondering if she was to put "the birthday" in that small box.

"Look, Missie," Clark told her, "look here in the box. This is fer Missie on her birthday."

He helped the child lift the top lid, and Missie stared in wonder at the item in the box. Clark lifted it out, wound it firmly, and placed it on the floor. When he released it, it began to spin, whirling out in many colors of red, blue, yellow, violet—too many to name.

Missie clasped her hands together excitedly, too awestruck to say anything.

When it stopped whirling she pushed it toward Clark, saying, "Do it 'gin."

Marty watched for some time before she turned to the dishes, and then suddenly she remembered her own gift. It certainly wasn't anything as delightful for a little girl as Clark's, she thought as she carried it from the bedroom. Maybe Missie wouldn't care for it at all. Well, she'd done what she could with what she had.

"Missie," she announced as she entered the kitchen, "I have somethin' fer ya, too," and she held out her gift.

"Well, I be," Clark muttered in astonished tones. "Missie, jest look what yer mama done made ya."

Marty knelt in front of the child and carefully fitted 'round her shoulders the small shawl over which she had labored. It was done in a soft blue, with pink rosebuds embroidered on it. Tassels lined the edge, and they seemed to especially intrigue the little girl, whose hands kept stroking them.

"Oh," said Missie. "Oh, Mama."

It was the first time she had used the term, and Marty found herself swallowing a lump in her throat. She tried to hide her feelings by adjusting the shawl to hang right.

Suddenly she was aware that Clark was looking at her, and there was a puzzled look on his face. Marty glanced down self-consciously and in so doing saw with horror the reason for the look. In kneeling before the child she had knelt on her skirt, pinning it down firmly so its tightness outlined her growing body. Flushing, she scrambled to her feet.

Now I've gone an' done it, she thought angrily. Well, she couldn't have gone on hiding it forever anyway. Besides, why should she feel any shame? It was Clem's baby, conceived in wedlock and love. She couldn't help that he was no longer here to share parenthood with her. Still, she didn't know why, but she just wished that this man who had taken her in didn't have to know about it until it had arrived. Well, there was no use fretting about it. He knew now and there was nothing she could be doing about it.

She turned to the dishes and Clark went back to playing with Missie.

Fifteen

Disclosed Secret

Next morning the sky was dark and scowling. The wind still blew from the north, telling the world it was now in charge. The horses huddled together, backs to the storm, and the cows gathered in the shelter of the barn, trying to escape the chill of the gale. Very few chickens appeared outside of the coop, and those that did soon dashed back to the warmth of the building. As Marty noted their flight from the blast, she remembered her resolve to speak to Clark about assuming the care of them.

"Dad-burn," she exclaimed under her breath, "I sure did pick me a grand time to be startin'."

Clark's prayer at breakfast that morning included a thanks to the Almighty for the warm shelter that was theirs, both for man and beast, and for the fact that they need not fear the cold of winter, due to the mercies of their great God. *An' to this hardworking man hisself,* added Marty mentally. However, she did acknowledge the truth found in the prayer. It was comforting to know they were prepared for the cold weather ahead.

Marty was just getting around to wondering once again what on earth she would do with Clark around the house all day, when he took her completely off guard.

"I be leavin' fer town right away," he said. "Is there anythin' thet ya be needin'?"

"But it's only Friday," Marty responded.

"Yes'm, I know thet, but I have some business there thet I'd like to be a seein' to right away like, an' if a storm comes up, we might jest have to sit tight a spell."

Marty couldn't help but feel the idea was a rather foolish one. This time he'd take a chill for sure. He'd managed to somehow sneak past his last tempting of fate without appearing any the worse for it, but surely he couldn't be that lucky again. But who was she to argue, and with a man? If they made up their minds, there just wasn't much a body could do about it. She left the table and checked out her list to see if anything else should be added.

Clark sat with his last sips of coffee, then finally spoke, his voice low. "Me bein' a man and all, I didn't notice what I s'pose a woman would have see'd long ago. I had me no idea thet ya was expectin' a young'un."

Marty did not look up from her list. She did not want to meet his eyes.

"I'm right sorry thet I didn't know. I might have saved ya some of the harder things. From now on, ya'll do no more totin' of them heavy water pails. When ya be needin' extra water fer washin' an' sech, ya be lettin' me know."

How silly, thought Marty. *If this baby gonna be harmed by totin' water, the damage be done long ago.*

But she said nothing, and Clark went on. "We be blessed with lots of good fresh milk. I hope ya be takin' advantage of it. If there be anythin' ya need or anythin' I can do, I'd be obliged if ya let me know."

He paused, then said, "Seein' as how I be goin' to town today anyhow, I figured as how maybe Mrs. McDonald would fix up a bundle of sewing pieces thet ya be needin' to sew baby things. If there be anythin' in particular thet ya be settin' yer mind on, then try to describe it fer her on the list."

Marty stood tongue-tied, and she felt her stomach knot. She hadn't gotten around to worrying yet how she would clothe the new young one. It had seemed so very far off in the future, but Clark was right. She must start sewing or she'd never be ready.

"Thank ya," she finally answered Clark. "I'm sure Mrs. Mc-Donald be knowin' better'n me what I be needin'," and she handed him the completed list.

She looked out of the window, still anxious about the weather. Storms came suddenly out here on the prairie some-times, she was told, and she hated to see Clark set out when there was a chance that one was on the way. He seemed to read her thoughts.

"Plenty of time to git to town an' back," he said. "Iffen a storm should catch me, there be plenty of neighbors livin' between here an' town, an' I'd be able to take shelter with one of them if I be needin' to."

"But . . . but what 'bout the chores?" Marty stammered. "I don't even know what to do, or where to find the feed, or nut-hin'."

Clark swung around to face her, and it was clear from the look on his face that he had not considered the question of her with the chores.

"Iffen a storm be comin' an' I have to shelter an' don't make it home, ya don't leave this house. Do ya hear?"

Marty heard, loud and clear.

"Don't ya worry none 'bout the hens or the hogs or even the milk cows. Nuthin'—I mean nuthin'—out there be so important thet I want ya out there in a storm tryin' ta care fer it."

So that's the way it be, thought Marty, hiding her smile. *Well, he needn't get so riled up 'bout it.*

It was the closest to upset she had ever seen Clark, and she couldn't help but be surprised. He turned from her, buttoned his heavy jacket, and reached for his mitts. He hesitated. "Might be a fine day to be a piecin' a quilt. The little feller will be a needin' a warm 'un."

Yeah, Marty thought, *he—or maybe she—most likely will.*

"I'll be back fer chore time," Clark assured her as he moved to go out the door; then he paused a moment and said quietly, "I be right glad thet ya'll have a little'un to remember 'im by"—and he was gone.

Sixteen

Thoughtful and Caring

Clark did return in time for the chores, much to Marty's relief. By then the snow was falling, swirling around angrily as it passed the window. Clark went right on down to the barn to take care of Dan and Charlie.

"He be settin' more stock on them horses than on his own self," Marty murmured to herself as she watched from the kitchen window. "He's been out in the weather as long as them two."

She moved to the stove and pushed the coffee closer to the center of the firebox so that it would be sure to be hot.

Missie had been playing on the floor, but when she heard Ole Bob's joyous bark of welcome, she jumped up, eyes shining.

"Daddy comin'," she said excitedly.

Marty smiled, noting again the fact that Missie often said "Daddy" even though Clark referred to himself as "Pa." Ellen must have preferred "Daddy," Marty decided. Well, then, for Ellen's sake, she would talk about Daddy to Missie, too.

Clark was soon in, arms full of bundles and face red from the cold wind. At the sight of her pa, Missie danced around wildly.

"Daddy here—Daddy here. Hi, Pa."

Clark called to her and, when he had rid himself of his parcels, swung the little girl up into his arms. She exclaimed over his cold face as she patted his cheeks.

"Best ya be warmin' up a bit 'fore ya start the chores," Marty suggested as she poured a cup of coffee.

"Sounds like a right good idea," he responded, taking off his heavy coat and hanging it by the fire to let it warm until he had to go out again. He stood for a moment with his hands over the stove and then crossed to the table. Marty poured cream in the coffee and placed it before him.

"Thet there fair-sized bundle be yourn," Clark said. "Mrs. McDonald was right excited 'bout fixin' it up. Think she was a mite confused. Seemed to think it was my young'un. It bein' none of her business, I didn't bother none to set her straight."

He swallowed a few more gulps of hot coffee. Marty's thoughts whirled.

His young'un? How could it be his young'un, us not even bein' true man an' wife? 'Course, Mrs. McDonald wouldn't be knowin' thet. She felt her face coloring in embarrassment.

Clark put down his cup and calmly continued, "I got ta thinkin' later, though, thet maybe I should've said somethin', so I went back. 'Mrs. McDonald,' I says, 'true, my missus be havin' a young'un, and true I'll be a treatin' it as one of mine, but also true thet the pa be her first husband an' thet bein' important to her, I wouldn't want folks gettin' things mixed up like.'"

Clark finished his coffee. "Well, I best be gettin'."

He shrugged into his coat and was gone before Marty had time to get her scrambling thoughts in order.

He understood. He'd gone back to the store to set Mrs. McDonald straight because he knew, as Ma Graham had told Marty, that her tongue was the busiest part of her anatomy. Give the woman a day or two of fair weather and everyone in the area would know of the coming baby.

Clark understands that it be important to me that the new baby be known as Clem's. Her mind continued to try to sort out this man as she began to put away the supplies he had purchased.

She turned with anticipation to her bundle and decided to take it in on her bed to examine the contents. It was cold in the bedroom now, and she shivered, partly from excitement, she was sure, as she unwrapped the brown store paper.

Mrs. McDonald certainly had gone all out. Marty's hands went to her face as she looked at the beautiful materials. Surely a young'un didn't need that many baby things. Her cheeks flushed at the thought of the days and evenings ahead when she could sit and work on the small garments. She wished she had someone to talk with about her feelings and was tempted to pour it all out on Missie. No, she'd best wait awhile for that. The remaining months would seem far too long for a two-year-old. Oh, if only Clem were here to share it with her. Her eyes filled once again, and a hot tear trickled down. She brushed it away with the back of her hand. If only it were that easy to get rid of the pain in her heart.

When Clark came in to supper, he was noticeably shivering in spite of his heavy coat. He remarked that he couldn't believe how much the temperature had dropped in a few short hours. The wind no doubt had a great deal to do with it, he added.

Before he sat down to the table, he lit the fireplace in the sitting room.

"Guess it's time," he observed, "to be havin' more heat than jest the cook stove."

When he prayed that night, he asked God to be with "people less blessed than we," and Marty was reminded of her covered wagon with the broken wheel. She shivered to think of what it would be like to be huddled in it now, trying to keep warm under their scant blankets.

After the meal Clark moved to the sitting room to check and replenish the fire, and Missie brought in her few toys to the rug in front of it.

Marty did the dishes, feeling warm and protected in spite of herself. How else could she feel in a snug cabin while the wind screamed around its corners, unable to get in?

The evening was still young, and Marty was anxious to get started on her sewing, but she realized how cold her room would be. She was still trying to figure out some answer to her problem as she emptied her dishpan and replaced it on its peg.

"It'll be right cold in yer room from now on," she heard Clark say from behind her. "Do ya be wantin' yer machine moved out to the sittin' room? There be plenty of room there fer it."

Marty turned and looked directly at him as she asked slowly, "Do ya mind seein' it sittin' there?"

"S'pose I do some," he answered frankly. "But it's not as hard now as it was at first sight of it, an' 'twould be only foolhardy not to put it where it can be of best use. I'll git used to it." So saying, he went to do as he had suggested.

Yes, Marty thought to herself, *this man will do the right thing even if it hurts.*

She felt a bit selfish about her anticipation of sewing in the warm room. If things had to be as they were, caught in a marriage she certainly would not have chosen on her own, she could have done worse. She still ached for her Clem. She wished him back, even if it meant having far less than what she had now. Still, she would be unfair if she refused to see the goodness in this man whose name she had taken and whose home she shared. That he was a real worker and a good provider was apparent, but she was discovering other things about him, too—things like thoughtfulness and caring. Certainly she couldn't fault him in his demands on her. She was only expected to be Missie's mama and to keep up the little home. He hadn't even complained about her cooking. No, she decided, even though she didn't like her situation, she could have done much worse.

She set her mind on her sewing. She would give Missie a bit more playing time before she tucked her in for the night. Clark had settled himself near the fireplace with one of his new books. Marty thankfully picked up a pattern that Mrs. McDonald had included. She had never sewed for one so small before and would have been hard put to know how to cut the material without the pattern. Her hands fairly trembled with excitement. She'd do the cutting on the kitchen table, where she had more room. She couldn't help but think the three of them seemed almost like a real family.

Seventeen

Mysterious Absence

The days of November brought more storms, and snow lay heavy on the fields and big drifts rose around sheltered spots. Occasionally the wind ceased blowing and the sun shone, but the temperature always stayed below freezing. There was still much to do, however, and activity on the small homestead did not cease because of the weather. Whenever the snowstorms abated, Clark hitched up the horses and spent his time with faithful Dan and Charlie in the wooded backcountry gathering logs for their fuel supply.

On the more miserable days, extra time spent in the barn eased the animals through the inclement weather with as little discomfort as possible.

Marty filled her days caring for Missie, keeping up the house, baking bread, washing, mending, ironing—the list seemed end-less to her, yet she was thankful to have each of the long days occupied, particularly ones that held her indoors.

In the evenings she went gladly to her sewing, adding each

stitch on the tiny garments with tender care. She had laid aside the quilt she had begun. It could wait. She wanted to concentrate on preparations for the baby.

She had noticed Clark often referred to the coming infant as "he." The baby could surprise them both and be a girl, she knew, but Marty was rather determined to think of a son for Clem.

She'd already decided on a name—Claridge Luke. Claridge after his pa's last name, and Luke in honor of her father. How proud her pa would be to know he had a grandson bearing his name. But that would have to wait for the first wagon train going east, when she'd pack up her son—maybe even Missie— and head back home.

The thought of taking Missie along with her was of more and more concern. What was best—both for the little girl and for Clark? She saw the great love Clark had for his daughter, and she wondered when the time came if he'd really be able to let her go. Or if he should. Marty herself was getting awfully attached to the child. Saying "Mama" came easy now to both of them. Indeed, sneaking up quite unawares was the feeling she was just that, Missie's mama. Each day she enjoyed the young child's company more, laughing at her silly antics, marveling at her new words, and even sharing some of them with Clark when he came home at night.

With Marty hardly realizing it, Missie was becoming very much a part of her life. She could barely wait for the new year, the time she had planned for telling her secret to the little girl. She was sure the child would share her anticipation of the new baby. But Marty didn't let herself stop to think too deeply about it all or to analyze her gradually changing feelings. It was enough just to tick the slow days off, discarding them casually like something that had served its purpose, and move forward; for indeed, Marty was still marking time.

As November drew to a close, Marty realized that Clark seemed to have made an unusual number of trips into town, especially for that time of year. It wasn't as though they had need of specific supplies. They had stocked up in preparation for winter's confining grip. And indeed Clark sometimes returned with very few purchases, even using the saddle horse on occasion rather than the team. Marty hadn't thought to wonder about it at first, but this morning's breakfast conversation had gotten her to puzzling over it. Clark had announced casually enough that he would be gone for three or four days. There appeared to be a break in the weather, he explained, so he had decided now was the time to make a trip to a town much larger than their small local one. Clark had arranged for young Tom Graham to come in the evening and stay the night to look after the evening and morning chores, he told her. If the weather should turn sour, Marty could ask him to stay on through the day, as well. If she was in need of anything, she could send word with Tom to the Grahams.

His words had puzzled Marty. He indeed had taken an unusual number of trips, now that she thought about it, but really it was none of her business. He was probably looking for new machinery to till the land, or better seed, or a place to sell his hogs. Anyway, it was his doings, so why should she worry over it? Young Tom would be over. There was nothing further with which to concern herself.

Still, as Clark gave Missie a good-bye hug and admonished her to be a good girl for her mama, Marty couldn't help but feel at least curious and maybe a bit uneasy.

"I'll be back Saturday night in time fer chores," he promised and went to the barn for Dan and Charlie. As Marty watched him leave the yard, she noticed that the crate was in the wagon box and a couple of hogs were having a ride along to town.

What had he said a while ago? *"If we be needin' more cash, we can al'ays sell a hog."*

He must be shoppin' for 'nother plow or more seed, she decided with a shrug. Still, on the other hand, she had cost him a powerful lot of extra money, what with the winter clothing for herself, the wool for knitting and the pieces for quilting, and then to top it off, the things for the baby.

Marty fretted over the realization, something she usually kept herself from doing. Finally, with real effort she pushed it aside.

"No use takin' on so," she murmured to herself. "Guess I'm jest a mite off my feed or somethin' to be stewin' 'bout it so. Wish I could have me a good visit with Ma. Thet'd set things to right. By the time Clark gits back, it'll be December already."

Time was indeed moving on, no matter how slow it could seem, and hadn't Ma said that it was time that healed? She hoped the days would go quickly while Clark was away.

Marty was more relieved than she would admit to see the team coming on Saturday as the sun was setting. She didn't know why she should feel that way. Young Tom had done a fine job of the chores, she was sure, and she hadn't at all minded his company in the evenings. After supper he played with Missie or read and reread her book to her. He was proud of the fact that he had learned his letters and knew how to read, as did each of Ma's children. He loved to show off to Missie and—Marty smiled—to her, as well, she wagered. By now Missie could repeat many of the lines of her book and loved to pretend she was reading herself.

They had gotten along just fine while Clark was away, so that had no bearing on her sense of relief to see him come home. Perhaps deep within was the haunting memory of a casual good-bye to Clem and a later discovery that it had been the last, but she shook off that possibility and went to tell Missie that her pa was home.

Missie was overjoyed at the sight of her daddy and began a dance as soon as she spotted him from the chair at the window.

Marty noticed the crate was now empty, but she could see no purchase that might have been made from the proceeds. Only a few small packages sat on the seat beside Clark. Dan and Charlie looked weary, she thought, as she watched them plod toward the barn, but their steps picked up as they drew near warm stalls and a full manger.

Clark looks tired, too, she decided as she watched him climb down and begin to unhitch the team. He wasn't moving with the same energy that usually accompanied his activities.

"Well, your pa's here now an' he'll be wantin' some hot coffee," Marty remarked as she helped Missie down from her perch at the window.

Coffee presented no problem, for Marty had it at the ready. She had made it in between her pacings back and forth to the window watching for the first glimpse of the team.

Things, she hoped, would continue on now in their usual way. This wasn't the life she had wanted or planned, but at least her days had taken on a pattern now familiar to her, and there was a certain amount of comfort in the familiar.

Clark came in with a few groceries, and Marty welcomed him with a cup of coffee and a happy little girl to greet him.

Eighteen

Christmas Preparations

"Our God," Clark addressed the Almighty in his morning prayer, "as we be nearin' the season of yer Son's birth, make our hearts thankful thet He came, an' help us to be lovin' our neighbor with a love like He showed us."

He's talkin' 'bout Christmas, Marty thought with a sudden awareness of the season. *Oh my, it be only two weeks away, an' I haven't even been thinkin' on it.*

Her mind went plunging from thought to thought, so again she had missed the rest of the prayer and sat with eyes still closed after the "amen." Missie pulled at her sleeve, wanting her breakfast.

Marty lifted a flushed face and hurriedly fixed Missie's porridge for her, blowing on it to cool it before giving it to the child.

"Ya know," she ventured a little later, "I had fergot all 'bout how close Christmas be."

Clark looked up from his own bowl of porridge. "I know Christmas be a mite hard to be a thinkin' on this year. Iffen it be too hard fer ya, we can most ferget the day, 'cept fer the reading of the Story an' maybe a sock fer young Missie."

Marty thought for a few minutes.

"No," she finally answered. "Thet wouldn't be right. Missie needs her Christmas—a proper one like, an' I reckon it may do us good, too. We can't stay back in the past nursin' our sorrow—not for her sake, nor fer our own. Christmas, seems to me, be a right good time to lay aside hurtin' an' look fer somethin' healin'."

Clark stared at her for a while, then dropped his eyes back to his bowl. He finally said quietly, "Seems I never heard a better sermon from any visitin' preacher than the one I jest heard." He paused a moment, then said, "Ya be right, of course. So what ya be plannin'?"

"Well . . ." Marty turned it over in her mind, trying to recall exactly what had happened at her home to prepare for Christmas. There hadn't been the reading of the Scripture story, but they could add that easy enough. And there had been a good supply of corn liquor, which they could do without. Otherwise, there must be several things she could do the way her mother had. This would be her first Christmas away from home—the first Christmas for her to make for others, rather than have others make for her. The thought made her feel both uneasy and excited.

"Well," she began again, "I'll git me to doin' some Christmas bakin'. Maybe Ma has some special recipes she'll share. Then we'll have a tree fer Missie. Christmas Eve we'll put it up after she be tucked in, an' we'll string popcorn an' make some colored chains, an' have a few candles fer the windows, an' we'll kill a couple of the finest roosters, an' I'll find me somethin' to be makin' fer Missie—"

The excitement growing in her must have been infectious. Clark joined in with his own anticipation of the coming Christmas.

"Roosters, nuthin'," he announced. "I'll go myself an' buy us a turkey from the Vickers. Mrs. Vickers raises some first-rate 'uns. Maybe there be somethin' we can be makin' fer Missie together. I'll ride over to Ma's today an' git the recipes—or better still, it looks like a decent day. Ya be wantin' me to hitch ole Dan an' Charlie so ya can be goin' yerself?"

"Oh, could I?" Marty's tone held the plea in her heart. "I'd love to see Ma fer a chat—iffen yer sure it be all right."

So it was decided that Marty would go to the Grahams'. But Clark added another dimension to the plan. If it was okay with her, he'd drive her to Ma's, and then he and Missie would go on to the Vickers's and get the turkey. That way they'd be sure to have it when the big day arrived. Missie could do with some fresh air, too, and some time with her pa.

Marty hurried through the dishes as Clark went to get the team. She bundled Missie up snugly and slipped into her long coat. It was the first time she had worn it, and she thought, looking at herself with a grin, perhaps the last for a while. Two of the buttons refused to meet their matching buttonholes. She sighed. "Well," she told Missie, taking her shawl, "guess I'll jest have to cover up the rest o' me with this."

The day spent with Ma was a real treat. They pored over Ma's recipes, Marty selecting so many that she'd never get them all baked. She would choose some from among the many at a later date. She also wrote down careful instructions on how to stuff and roast the turkey, it being her first attempt at such an endeavor. They shared plans and discussed possibilities for the holiday ahead. Marty felt a stirring of new interest within her at the anticipation of it. For too long she had felt that the young life she carried was the only living part of her. Now for the first time in months she began to feel alive again.

Before she knew it, she heard the team approaching. Clark was called in for a cup of coffee before setting off for home, and he came in carrying a rosy-faced Missie, excited by her ride and eager to tell everyone of the "gobble-gobble" they had in the wagon for "Christ'as."

Marty could hear the live turkey vigorously protesting his separation from the rest of the flock. Clark had said he would be placed in the hens' coop and generously given cracked corn and other fattening things until a few days before Christmas.

Missie romped with young Lou while the grown-ups had their coffee, too excited to even finish her glass of milk.

On the way home Marty got up the nerve to voice a thought that had gradually been taking shape. She was a bit hesitant and hardly knew how to express it.

"Do ya s'pose—I mean, would ya mind iffen we had the Grahams come fer Christmas dinner?"

"All of 'em?" Clark's shock was evident.

"'Course, all of 'em," Marty rejoined stoutly. "I know there be thirteen of 'em an' three of us; thet makes sixteen. The kitchen table, stretched out like, will hold eight. Thet's the four grown-ups an' the four youngest of the Grahams. Missie'll be in her chair. Thet leaves seven Graham young'uns. We'll fix 'em a place in the sittin' room an' Laura an' Sally Anne can look after 'em."

She would have babbled on, but Clark, with a laugh and an upright hand, stopped her. "Whoa." Then he said, "I see ya got it all sorted out. Did ya speak with Ma on it?"

"'Course not," said Marty. "I wouldn't be doin' thet afore I checked with you."

He looked sideways at her, and his voice took on a serious note. "I don't know." He hesitated. "Seems to me it be a pretty big order, gettin' on a Christmas dinner fer sixteen, an' servin' it in our small quarters, an' ya bein' the way ya are an' all."

Marty knew she must fight for it if her idea was to be.

She scoffed at his protest. "Pawsh! There be nuthin' wrong with the way I be. I feel as pert now as I ever did. As to fixin' the dinner, I'll have as much of thet done ahead as I can, afore the house packs jam tight. Then 'twon't be sech a problem. When they gits there, Ma and the girls will give a hand—an' with the dishes, too. Oh my—"

She stopped and fairly squealed. "Dishes! Clark, do we have enough dishes to set so many?"

"I don't know, but iffen ya don't, Ma'll bring some of hers along."

"Good!"

She smiled to herself. He had as good as said that they could come. She had sort of swung him off track by diverting his attention to the dishes. She felt a bit guilty but not enough to be bothered by it. "It be settled, then," she ventured, more a statement than a question.

Nineteen

Snowbound

Clark went back to his days in the hills felling trees, and Marty went to work in her kitchen. She pored over the recipes and, after finally making her choices, spent day after day turning out tempting goodies. In spite of Missie's attempts to "help," baked goods began to stock up almost alarmingly, and she was having a hard time finding places to put all of them.

Missie sampled and approved, preferring the gingerbread boys Marty had made especially for the children.

In the evenings she and Clark worked together on a dollhouse for Missie. Clark had constructed a simple two-room structure and was busy making wooden chairs, tables, and beds. Marty's part was to put in small curtains, rugs, and blankets. "Those things a woman usually be makin'," Clark had said. She found it to be fun helping with the project, watching it take shape. The kitchen had a small cupboard with doors that really opened, a table, two chairs, and a bench. This was Clark's work. Marty had put up little kitchen curtains, added a couple of bright rugs on the floor, and put small cushions on the chairs.

The sitting-bedroom had a small bed complete with blankets and pillows, a tiny cradle, two chairs, a footstool, and a trunk with a lid that lifted. Marty still had to fix the blanket and pillow for the cradle and the curtains for this room. Clark was working on a stove for the kitchen.

"Wouldn't be much of a kitchen without a stove," he reasoned.

Marty was pleased with their efforts and glad that the dollhouse should easily be finished in time for Missie's Christmas.

Clark had made several more trips into town, stopping the first time to invite the Grahams to Christmas dinner. He seemed to feel these trips were important, yet as far as Marty could see, he had nothing to show for them when he returned. She shrugged it off.

The last time he had brought back some special spices for her baking and a few trinkets for Missie.

"She be needin' somethin' fer her Christmas sock," he said as he handed them over to Marty's care.

Marty reviewed all this in her thinking as she laid cookies out to cool.

Would Clark be expecting a gift from her? She supposed not. It would have been nice to have some little thing for him, but she had no money for a purchase and no way of getting someplace to buy it. And what could one sew for a man?

As she worked she remembered the piece of soft blue-gray wool that still lay in her sewing basket. After she finished the cookies, she'd take a look at it and see if it were possible to make a man's scarf out of the material.

When she later checked the material, she decided it was quite possible. Knowing that Clark wouldn't be in from cutting trees until chore time, she set to work. She finished the stitching, finding it necessary to do a bit of piecing, and then tucked it away. Tomorrow while Clark was away she would hand embroider his initials on it.

Christmas would soon be here. She wondered if the day itself would be half as exciting as the preparations for it had been.

Only three days to go now. They had finished their gift for Missie the night before and complimented each other on the outcome. Now breakfast was over, and Clark had gone back to cutting wood. Marty asked him to keep an eye open for nice pine branches bearing cones so she might form a few wreaths. He said he would see what he could do.

Clark would work in the morning in the hills, and in the afternoon he would kill the gobbler, who at the present was going without his breakfast. Marty hurried through her tasks, then took up the scarf for Clark. Carefully she stitched a bold C. D. on it and had it tucked away in her drawer before Clark arrived for dinner.

Now just two days until Christmas, but the day was the Lord's Day, and any further preparations would have to wait. Marty conceded to herself that perhaps a day of rest was not such a bad idea, and when Missie was tucked in for her afternoon nap, she stretched out on her own bed, a warm blanket drawn over her. She felt weary, really weary, and the weight of the baby she carried made every task she took on doubly hard. She closed her eyes and gave herself up to a delightful sleep.

Day one—the morrow would be Christmas. The tom was killed, plucked, cleaned, and hung to chill in preparation for stuffing. Marty had carefully formed her wreaths, pleased with Clark's selected branches, and tied them with her cherished store twine. She had placed one in each window and one on the door. A small tree had come from the hills with Clark's last load of wood and waited outside until the time when Missie would be tucked in bed and it would be placed in a corner of the sitting room. The corn already had been popped and strung, and Marty had made chains from bits of colored paper that she had carefully saved. She had even made some out of the brown store wrap that had come from town.

The scarf lay completed, but as Marty looked at it a feeling of uneasiness overtook her. Somehow it didn't seem the thing to be giving a man like Clark. She wondered if she'd really have the courage to go through with it.

Well, she said, mentally shelving the matter, *I'll have to be handlin' thet when the time comes, an' jest keep my mind on what I'm doin' now.*

What she was "doin' now" was peeling large quantities of carrots, turnips, and potatoes for the Christmas dinner. There would be cabbage to dice, as well. The batch of bread was rising and would soon be ready for baking. The beans were soaking and would be flavored with cured ham later. Canned greens and pickles were lined up on the floor by the cupboard, waiting to be opened, and wild nuts were placed in a basket by the fireplace to be roasted over the open fire.

Mentally Marty ticked off her list. Things seemed to be going as scheduled. She looked around her at the abundance of food. Tomorrow promised to be a good day, and tonight they'd have the fun of decking the tree for Missie and hanging her sock.

Christmas Day! Marty opened her eyes earlier than usual, and already her head was spinning. She must prepare the stuffing for the turkey, put the vegetables on to cook in her largest kettles, bring in plenty of the baking from the shed, where it was sure to be frozen in this weather. Her mind raced on as she quickly dressed.

The room felt so cold she'd be glad to get to the warm kitchen. She silently bent over Missie to check that she was properly covered, then quietly tiptoed from the room.

It was cold in the sitting room, too, and she hurried on to the kitchen. There was no lamp lit there, so Clark was not up. She shivered as she hastened to light it and moved on to start the fire. It was so cold that her hands already felt numb. She could hear the wind whining around the cabin as she coaxed the blaze to take hold. It would be a while before the chill left the air. She moved into the sitting room to light the fire there. She must have it warm when Missie got up.

When both fires were burning, she checked the clock. Twenty minutes to six. No wonder Clark wasn't up yet. He usually rose about six-thirty in the winter months. Well, she needed every minute she could get. She had so much to do.

She turned to the frost-covered window and scratched a small opening with her fingers to look out on Christmas Day. An angry wind swirled heavily falling snow, piling drifts in seemingly mountainous proportions. She could not even see the well for the density of it.

Marty didn't need to be told that she was witnessing a dreaded prairie blizzard. The pain of it all began to seep in. She wanted to scream out against it, to curse it away, to throw herself on her bed in a torrent of tears. Her shoulders sagged and she felt weary and defeated. But what good would it do to strike back? The storm would still rage. None in their right mind would defy it simply for a Christmas dinner. She was licked. She felt dead again. Then suddenly a new anger took hold of her. Why? Why should the storm win?

"Go ahead," she stormed aloud as she stared out through the window. "Go ahead and howl. We have the turkey ready to go in the oven. We have lots of food. We have our tree. We have Missie. We'll—we'll jest still have Christmas!"

She wiped angry tears on her apron, squared her shoulders, and turned back to add more wood to the fire. Then she noticed Clark sitting there, boots in hand, watching her.

He cleared his throat, and she looked steadily at him. She had worked so hard for this day and now she was cheated out of it. She hoped he would not try to say something understanding or her resolve might crumble. She quickly moved to stand in front of him as he sat lacing his boots, and with a smile she waved her hand toward the laden cupboard. "My word. What're we ever gonna be doin' with all this food? We'll have to spend the whole day eatin' on it."

She moved back to the cupboard and began work on preparing the turkey for roasting.

"I do hope thet the Grahams haven't been caught short-fixed fer Christmas. Us sittin' here with jest us three an' all this food, an' them sittin' there with so many. . . ." She drifted to a halt and glanced over at Clark, who sat there openmouthed, a boot dangling from his hand.

He shook his head slightly, then said, "Ma's too smart to be took off guard like. She knows this country's mean streak. I don't think they be a wantin' at all."

Marty felt relieved at that news. "I be right glad to hear thet," she said. "The storm had me worryin'."

She finished stuffing the turkey, then opened the oven door.

"Best ya let me be liftin' thet bird. He's right heavy," Clark said and hurried over to put it in.

Marty did not object. With it safely roasting and the stove gradually warming the kitchen, Marty put on the coffeepot and then took a chair.

"Seems the storm nearly won," she acknowledged slowly, "but it can't win unless ya let it, can it?"

Clark said nothing, but as she looked at him his eyes told her that he understood her disappointment—and more than that, her triumph over it.

He reached out and touched her hand. When he spoke his voice was gentle. "I'm right proud of ya, Marty."

He had never touched her before except for helping her in and out of the wagon, and something about it sent a warm feeling through her. Maybe it was knowing that he understood. She hoped he hadn't noticed her response to his touch and quickly said, "We'll have to cook the whole turkey, but we can freeze what we can't eat. I'll put the vegetables in smaller pots an' cook only what we be needin'. The rest will keep fer a while in the cold pit. The bakin'"—she stopped and waved a hand to all the goodies stacked around and laughed—"we be eatin' thet till spring iffen we don't git some help."

"Thet's one thing I don't be complainin' 'bout," Clark said. "Here I was worryin' 'bout all those Graham young'uns with their hefty appetites comin' an' not leavin' anythin' fer me, an' now look at me, blessed with it all."

"Clark," Marty said in mock dismay, "did you go an' pray up this storm?"

She'd never heard him laugh so heartily before, and she joined in with him. By then the coffee was boiling, and she poured two cups while he went for the cream. The kitchen was warmer now, and the hot coffee washed away the last of the chill in her.

"Well," she said, getting up as quickly as her extra burden would allow, "we may as well have some bakin' to go with it. Gotta git started on it sometime. What ya be fancyin'?"

Clark chose a spicy tart and Marty took a simple shortbread cookie.

They talked of the day ahead as they shared their coffee. Clark wouldn't go out for the chores until after Missie was up. That way he wouldn't miss out on her excitement. Then they would have a late breakfast and their Christmas dinner midafternoon. The evening meal would be "the pickin's," Clark said. That would save Marty from being at the stove all day. It sounded like a reasonable plan to her, and she nodded her agreement.

"We used to play a game when I was a kid," Clark said. "Haven't played a game fer years, but it might be fun. It was drawed out on a piece o' paper or a board, an' ya used pegs or buttons. While ya be busyin' about, I'll make us up one."

The clock ticked on and the snow did not cease nor the wind slacken, but it didn't matter now. It had been accepted as a fact of prairie life, and the adjustments had been made.

When Missie called from her bed, Clark went for her. Marty stationed herself by the sitting room fire to watch the little girl's response to their Christmas preparations. They were not disappointed. Missie was beside herself with excitement. She rushed to the tree, went from the small toys in her sock to the dollhouse, then to the sock, back to the dollhouse, exclaiming over and over her wonder of it all. Finally she stopped, clasped her tiny hands together, and said, "Oh, Chris'as bootiful."

Clark and Marty laughed. She was off again, kneeling before the dollhouse, handling each small item carefully as she took it out and placed it back again.

Clark finally stood reluctantly to go do the chores. The storm was still raging, and he dressed warmly against it. Caring for the stock would be difficult on such a day, and he murmured to Marty that he was glad the animals were sheltered from the wind.

Marty felt some concern as she watched him go out. The snow was so thick at times that you couldn't see the barn. She was glad he took Ole Bob with him, as the dog could sense directions should the storm confuse Clark. He also left instructions with her. If he wasn't in by midmorning, she was to fire the gun into the air and repeat, if necessary, at five-minute intervals. Marty fervently hoped it wouldn't be necessary.

Much to Marty's relief, Clark was in before the appointed time, chilled by the wind but reporting all things in order.

She put the finishing touches on breakfast, and they sat down to eat. Missie could hardly bear to leave her new toys and came only with repeated promises that she could return to them following the meal.

They all bowed their heads and Clark prayed. "Sometimes, Lord, we be puzzlin' 'bout yer ways. Thank ya, Lord, thet the storm came well afore the Grahams be settin' out. We wouldn't want 'em caught in sech a one."

Marty hadn't thought of that, but she totally agreed.

"An', Lord, thank ya fer those who share our table, an' bless this day of yer Son's birth. May it be one thet we can remember with warm feelin's even if the day be cold. Thank ya, Lord, fer this food thet ya have provided by yer goodness. Amen."

"Amen," said Missie, then she looked up at her pa. "The house"—she pointed—"thanks—house."

Clark looked puzzled. Marty, too, felt bewildered but tried to understand what the small child meant.

"I believe she be wantin' ya to say thanks fer her dollhouse," Marty finally ventured.

"Is thet it? Okay, Missie, we pray again. An' thank ya, Lord, fer Missie's dollhouse. Amen."

Missie was satisfied, and after her second "amen," she quickly began work on her breakfast between quick glances over at the beloved dollhouse.

They roasted nuts at the open fire, played the game Clark had made, which Marty won with alarming consistency, and watched Missie at her play. When the child was later tucked in for a nap, a tiny doll chair firmly grasped in hand, Marty got busy with the final dinner preparations. After the child awoke they would have their Christmas dinner. She wanted everything to be just right. From those early days of only pancakes to a bountiful table spread with all manner of good things in just a little over two months. Marty was rather pleased with herself.

After they had eaten more than enough of the sumptuous meal, Clark suggested they read the Christmas story in the sitting room while their food settled.

"Yer turnin' out to be a right fine cook," he observed, and Marty could feel herself flush at the compliment. "I think Ma

Graham would be even more impressed than me," he went on, "and we'll jest have to plan us another get-together so she can find out fer herself."

They moved to the sitting room, and Clark took Missie on his knee and opened the Bible. He first read of the angel appearing to the young girl, Mary, telling her that she had been chosen as the mother of the Christ child. He went on to read of Joseph and Mary's trip to Bethlehem, where no room was found in the inn, so that night the infant Jesus was born in a stable and laid in the cattle's manger. The shepherds heard the good news from the angels and rushed to see the newborn king. Then the wise men came, following the star and bearing their gifts to the child, going home a different way for the protection of the baby.

Marty thought she had never heard anything so beautiful. She couldn't remember ever knowing the complete story before as it was given in the Scriptures. A little baby born in a stable was God's Son. She placed a hand over her own little one.

Wouldn't be carin' fer my son to be born in a barn, she thought. *Don't suppose God was wantin' it thet way, either, but no one had room fer a wee baby. Still—God did watch over Him, sendin' angels to tell the shepherds an' all. An' the wise men, too, with their rich gifts. Yes, God was carin' 'bout His Son.*

The story captured Marty's imagination as she waited for the birth of her own first child, and she thought on it as she did the dishes. After she was through in the kitchen she returned to the sitting room. Clark had gone out to do the evening chores before it got too dark. It was hard enough to see one's way in the daylight in such a storm.

Marty sat down and picked up the Bible. She wished she knew where to locate the Christmas story so she might read it again, but as she turned the pages she couldn't find where Clark had read. She did find the Psalms, though, and read one after the other as she sat beside the warm fire. Somehow they were comforting, even when you didn't understand all of the phrases and ideas, she thought.

She read until she heard Clark entering the shed and then laid the Book aside. She'd best put on the coffee and get those "pickin's" ready.

Later that evening, after Missie had been put to bed, Marty got up the courage to ask Clark if he'd mind reading "the story" again. As he read, she sat trying to absorb it all. She knew a bit more about it this time, so she could follow with more anticipation, catching things she had missed the first time. She fleetingly wondered if Clem had ever heard all of this. It was such a beautiful story.

Oh, Clem! her heart cried. *I wish I coulda shared sech a Christmas with you.* But it was not to be, and Marty took a deep breath and concentrated on the story from the Book.

After the reading, Marty sat in silence, only her knitting needles clicking, for she did not enjoy idleness, even on Christmas.

Clark put the Bible away and went out to the lean-to. He returned with a small package.

"It ain't much," he said, looking both sheepish and expectant at the same time, "to be sayin' thank ya fer carin' fer Missie an' all."

Marty took it from him with a slight feeling of embarrassment. Fumbling, she took off the wrapping to reveal a beautiful dresser set, with ivory comb, brush, and hand mirror. Hand-painted flowers graced the backs in pale golds and rusts. It nearly took Marty's breath away.

She turned the mirror over in her hand and noticed letters on the handle, M.L.C.D. It took a minute for her to realize they were her initials: Martha Lucinda Claridge Davis. He had not only given her the set, he had given her back her name. Tears pushed out from under her lids and slid down her cheeks.

"It's beautiful," she whispered, "really beautiful an' I . . . I jest don't know how to thank ya."

Clark seemed to understand what had prompted the tears, and he nodded slowly.

Marty went to put the lovely set on her chest in her room. She remembered the scarf. She lifted it out of the drawer and looked at it. No, she decided. She just couldn't. It wouldn't do. She shoved it back in the drawer. It just wasn't good enough, she decided. Not good enough at all.

Twenty

A Visit from Ma Graham

Thinking back, Marty declared it a good Christmas in spite of having to overcome her keen disappointment. It would have been so much fun to have shared it with the Grahams, but as she had concluded there was nothing that could be done about that, somehow she felt sure Clark's prayer had been answered and that in years to come they would remember it with warm feelings.

After the storm, the wind stopped howling and the sun came out. The stock moved about outside again, and the chickens ventured from their coop to their wire enclosure for a bit of exercising. Ole Bob ran around in circles, glad to stretch his legs. Marty envied him as she watched. How good it would be to feel light and easy moving.

Looking carefully at herself for the first time in months, she studied her arms and hands. They were thinner than they used to be, she realized. She hiked up her skirt and looked at her legs. Yes, she definitely had lost weight, except for the one spot where she decidedly had put it on. She'd have to eat up a bit, she chided herself. She'd been quite thin enough before. After the baby arrived, she'd "blow away in the wind iffen she wasn't tied down," as her pa used to say. Well, she was sure enough tied down now, she concluded. The baby seemed to be getting heavier every day. She felt bulky and clumsy, a feeling she wasn't used to. Well, she realized, it was to be expected. December was as good as spent. Even as she thought of that, the month of January stretched out before her, looking oh so long. She wondered if she could endure it. Well, she'd just have to take it one day at a time.

January dawned with a bright sky and no wind, something Marty had learned to be thankful for. She hated the wind, she decided. It sent chills right through her.

This was the new year. What did it hold for her? A new baby for sure. Then a faint anxiety pressed upon her, and she implored Clark's God to please, please let everything be all right.

Clark had been to town again the day before and returned home with a rather grim expression. Marty was about to ask the meaning of all of the trips but checked her tongue.

Iffen it be somethin' I be needin' to know, he'd be sayin' so, she told herself as she went to get the breakfast on the table.

Seems on a new day of a new year, somethin' good should be happenin'.

When she checked out the kitchen window, she felt that it truly had, for there were three graceful and timid deer crossing the pasture. Marty ran back to the bedroom for Missie.

"Missie," she roused the little girl, "come see."

She hurried back to the kitchen, hoping the deer hadn't already disappeared. They had stopped and were grazing in an area where horses had pawed the snow from the grass.

"Look, Missie," Marty said, pointing.

"Oh-h," Missie's voice expressed her excitement. "Doggies."

"No, Missie," Marty giggled, "it's not doggies. It be deer."

"Deer?"

"That's right. Ain't they pretty, Missie?"

"Pretty."

As they watched, Clark came in from the barn, Ole Bob bounding ahead of him, barking at whatever took his fancy. The deer became instantly alert, long necks stretched up, legs tensed, and then, as though on a given signal, they all three leaped forward in long, graceful strides, lightly up and over the pasture fence and back into their native woods. It was a breathtaking sight, and Marty and Missie were still at the window gazing after them when Clark entered.

"Pa!" cried Missie, pointing. "Deer—they jump."

"So ya saw 'em, eh?"

"Weren't they somethin'?" Marty said in awe.

"They be right nice, all right, though they be a nuisance, too. Been noticing their tracks gettin' in closer an' closer. Wouldn't wonder that one mornin' I be a findin' 'em in the barn with the milk cows."

Marty smiled at his exaggeration. She finally pulled herself away from the window and busied herself with breakfast.

Later in the day, after the dinner dishes had been cleared away and Marty was putting some small stitches on a nightie for the new baby, she heard Ole Bob suddenly take up barking again. Someone was coming, she decided, and him not a stranger. She crossed to the window and looked down the road.

"Well, my word," she exclaimed, "it be Ma an' Ben!"

Joy filled her as she put aside her sewing and ran to make them welcome.

Clark came in from the yard, seeming not too surprised. He and Ben took the horses to the barn for sustenance and rest after their hard labor to buck some large drifts across the road. The two men then seated themselves in the sitting room by the fire and talked of next spring's planting and of their plans to extend their fields, and other man-talk.

Imagine thinkin' of plantin' now with ten-foot drifts standin' on the cornfields, Marty thought as she put on the coffee.

The women settled in the kitchen. Ma had brought along some knitting, and Marty brought out the sock she was knitting for Clark. She needed help in shaping the heel and was glad for Ma's guidance.

They discussed their Christmases and their disappointment, but both admitted to having a good Christmas in spite of it all. Ma remarked that they were more than happy to say yes when Clark had stopped by yesterday, inviting them to come for coffee New Year's Day if the weather held.

So thet's it, Marty thought. *An' he didn't tell me fer fear it might be ruined agin by "mean" weather, as he calls it.*

The visit took on even more meaning for her. Ma told Marty the news that young Jason Stern was there "most ever' time I turn me round." With misty eyes she told how Jason had come Christmas Eve and asked permission for Sally Anne and him to be "a marryin' when the preacher come for his spring visit."

"He seems a right good young man," she added, "an' I should feel proud like, but somehow it be hard to give up my Sally, her not yet bein' eighteen, though she will be, jest by the marryin' time."

Marty thought back to her own tearful pleas, begging her ma and pa for permission to marry young Clem. She had been about the age of Sally Anne. She suddenly saw her own ma and pa in a different light. No wonder they were hesitant. They knew life could be hard. Still, she was glad she had those few happy, even though difficult, months with Clem.

"Thet Jason," Ma went on, "he already be cuttin' logs fer to build a cabin. Wants 'em ready fer spring so there can be a cabin raisin' an' a barn raisin', too. Workin' right hard he is, an' his pa's a helpin' him. He's gonna farm the land right next to his pa. Well, we couldn't say no, Ben an' me, but we sure gonna miss her happy ways an' helpin' hands. I think it be troublin' Laura, too. She jest not been herself the last few days. Moody an' far off like. She always was a quiet one, but now she seems all locked up in herself like. Bothers me, it does."

Ma stopped and seemed to look at something a long way off. Then she pulled her attention back to the present. "We's all gotta settle in an' add to Sally Anne's marriage things—quilts an' rugs an' sech. Got a heap to do 'twixt now an' spring.

"How be things a comin' with the doc?" Ma asked, changing the subject and catching Marty completely off guard.

"What doc?" puzzled Marty.

"Why, the one Clark be a workin' on to git to come to town. The one he be makin' all the trips fer an' gettin' all the neighbors to sign up fer. He's most anxious like to git him here afore thet young'un of yourn makes his appearance."

At Marty's dumbfounded look, Ma finished lamely, "Hasn't he been tellin' ya?"

Marty shook her head.

"Hope I haven't spilled the beans," Ma said, "but ever'one

else in the whole West knows 'bout it, seems to me. Thought you'd be a knowin', too. But then maybe he thought it best ya not be gettin' yer hopes up. Might be ya jest not mention my big mouth to him, huh?" Ma Graham smiled a bit sheepishly, and Marty nodded her head, dumbly agreeing.

So that was it. All the urgent trips to town and sometimes beyond, even in poor weather, coming home cold and tired, to get a doctor to the area before her baby was due. She shook her head as she got up to put on the coffeepot. She had to move away quickly before Ma saw her tears.

Their morning coffee together was a sumptuous affair. Marty thought back to the time of Ma's first visit when all she could offer her was coffee. How different this was with the abundance of fresh bread and jelly, fancy cakes, tarts, and cookies. Ben remarked several times about her good cooking, and she responded that she should be—his cook had taught her. Missie wakened and joined them in her chair, asking for a gingerbread boy. Time passed all too quickly as they shared table and conversation.

Marty was reluctant to see them go but thankful for the unexpected time together, and she did want them to arrive home before nightfall.

After they had gone their way, she cheerfully began to clean up. She turned to Clark. "Thank ya so much fer invitin' them."

At his surprised look, she explained, "Ma let it slip, not knowin' thet I didn't know you had invited them." She couldn't resist adding, "I noticed, though, thet ya didn't invite all of those young'uns with the hearty appetites."

They shared a laugh together.

January's wintry days crawled by. Clark made more trips to

town, or wherever he went. Marty was no longer puzzled, and she felt quite sure he was going off on these cold days on her behalf. Her sewing was nearly completed now, and she looked at the small garments for her coming baby with much satisfaction. She would be so happy to be able to use the baby things, so new and sweet smelling.

Clark fretted about the lack of a cradle, and Marty assured him one wasn't needed yet as she planned to take the wee one into her bed until he grew a bit. Clark was satisfied with that, saying that come better weather he'd get busy on a bigger bed for Missie and let the baby take over her crib.

As the month drew to a close, Marty felt the time had come when she could share her secret with Missie. Clark had gone away again, and the two of them were alone in the house.

"Come with Mama, Missie," Marty said. "Mama wants to show ya somethin'."

Missie didn't have to be coaxed. She loved to be "showed somethin'." Together they went to the bedroom, where Marty lifted the stack of small garments from the drawer. She couldn't help but smile as she held the top one up for Missie to see.

"Look, Missie," she said. "These are fer the new baby. Mama's gonna get a new baby fer Mama and Missie. Jest a tiny little baby, only 'bout so big. Missie can help Mama take care of the baby."

Missie intently watched Marty's face. She obviously wasn't sure what this was all about, but Mama was happy, and if Mama was happy, it must be good.

"Ba-by," Missie repeated, stroking the soft things. "Ba-by, fer Mama—an' Missie?"

"Thet's right." Marty was wildly happy. "A baby fer Missie.

Look, Missie," she said, sitting on her bed, "right now the baby is sleepin' here."

She laid Missie's hand on her abdomen, and Missie was rewarded with a firm kick. Her eyes rose to Marty's in surprise as she quickly pulled away her hand.

"Thet's the baby, Missie. Soon the baby will sleep in Mama's bed. He'll come to live with Mama and Missie an' we'll dress 'im in these new clothes an' bundle 'im in these soft blankets, an' we can hold 'im in our arms, 'stead of how Mama be holdin' 'im now."

Missie didn't get it all, that was sure, but she could understand that Baby was coming and Mama was glad, and Baby would use the soft things and live in Mama's bed. Her eyes took on a sparkle. She touched Marty timidly and repeated, "Mama's ba-by."

Marty pulled the little girl to her and laughed with joy. "Oh, Missie," she said, "it's gonna be so much fun."

Clark returned home that night with a strange-looking lump under a canvas in the back of the sleigh.

Well, Marty thought wryly, *I'm sure thet be no doctor,* and her curiosity was sorely roused.

After Dan and Charlie had been fed and bedded, Clark came through the door carrying the surprise purchase.

Marty could scarcely believe her eyes. "A new rocking chair!" she exclaimed.

"Right," said Clark. "I vowed long ago thet iffen there ever be another baby in this house, there's gonna be a rockin' chair to quiet it by."

He grinned as he said it, and Marty knew the words really were a cover-up for other feelings.

"Well," she answered lightly, "best ya sit down an' show Missie how it works so you'll know how to use it when the baby's needin' ta be quieted." They shared a smile.

Then Clark pulled Missie up onto his lap and snuggled her close. They took two rocks, and the child popped up to stare at this wondrous thing. She watched, swaying, as Clark rocked a few more times, then settled back contentedly, enjoying the new marvel.

Clark soon had to leave for chores, and Missie crawled up on her own to try to make the chair respond correctly.

It's gonna be so much fun to have, Marty told herself. *Jest imagine me with my young'un all dressed up fancy like, an' me sittin' there rockin' 'im. Probably is room enough for Missie beside me, too. I can jest hardly wait.*

The baby seemed impatient, too, for it gave a hard kick that made its mother catch her breath and move back a mite from the cupboard where she was working.

When Clark came in from choring, Missie scooted down from the chair and ran to take his hand.

"Daddy, come," she urged him.

"Hold on, Missie, 'til yer pa gits his coat off," Clark laughed. "I'll come—I'll come."

Missie stepped back and watched him hang up his coat, then took his hand again. "Come see."

Marty thought she was still excited about the chair, and it looked like Clark assumed that, too, as he turned toward it. But Missie tugged at his hand to lead him over to Marty.

"Look—ba-by," she cried, pointing at the spot. "Ba-by fer Missie. Mama let Missie touch 'im."

Marty flushed and Clark grinned.

"Well, I reckon it be awful nice," he said, picking up the little girl. "So Missie's gonna git ta have a new baby, an' we'll rock 'im in the chair," he continued, walking away with the child as he spoke. "We'd better be gittin' some practice, don't ya s'pose. Let's rock a mite while yer mama gits our supper."

And they did.

Twenty-One

A New Baby

It was mid-February, and Marty sat opposite Clark at the table, both absorbed in their own thoughts. Clark's shoulders drooped, and Marty knew he probably was feeling discouraged over the outcome of all his efforts. A doctor indeed had been secured for the town and surrounding community, but he wouldn't be arriving until sometime in April. This was too late for what Clark—and Marty—had wanted him for.

Marty sat quietly, her own thoughts rather despondent. The little one was getting so heavy, and the last few days things just seemed different. She couldn't name what it was, but she knew it was there. She was troubled in her thinking. This was the time when a woman needed a "real" husband, one she could talk to. *If only Clem were here*—the eternal refrain again. She wouldn't have felt embarrassed to talk it over with Clem.

"I've been thinkin'," Clark interrupted her thoughts, "seems yer time must be gettin' perty close. Seems ya might feel more easy like iffen Ma could come a few days early an' be a staying' with ya fer a spell."

Marty hardly dared to hope. "Do ya really think she could?"

"Don't know why not. Sally Anne an' Laura be right able to care fer the rest. Good practice fer Sally Anne. Hear she be needin' to know all that afore long. I'll ride over an' have a chat with Ma. I hope we won't be keepin' her fer too long."

Oh, me too—me too. Marty's thoughts were a jumble of relief and concern. But she was so thankful for Clark's suggestion that she had to struggle to keep back the tears.

And so it was that Ma came that day, bringing with her a heavy feather tick and some quilts with which to make up a bed for herself on the sitting room floor. She was an old hand at this, and Marty took much comfort in her presence there.

Marty didn't keep her waiting long. Two mornings after, on February sixteenth, she awoke from a restless sleep sometime between three and four o'clock. She tossed and turned, not able to find a comfortable position, feeling generally uneasy.

What was uneasiness gradually changed to contractions— not too close and not too hard, but she recognized them for what they were. Around six o'clock Ma must have sensed more than heard her stirrings and came into her room to see how she was.

Marty groaned. "I jest feel right miser'ble," she muttered.

Ma gently laid a comforting hand on Marty's stomach and waited until another contraction seized her. "Good," she said. "They be nice an' firm. It be on the way."

Ma told Marty that she was going to make sure the fire that had been banked the night before was still alive. Marty could hear her put in more wood and fill the kettle and the large pot with water. "No harm in plenty of hot water," Ma said to Marty through the bedroom door. "It probably won't make an appearance for a while yet, but might as well be prepared." Her cheerful calm and obvious know-how were greatly assuring to Marty as another labor pain bore through her.

No doubt hearing some stirrings, Clark emerged from the lean-to. Even through her own distress, Marty could see that he was pale and already worried.

"Now, ya stop a frettin'," Marty heard Ma say to him. "I know thet she be a little thing"—her voice dropped a notch—"but she be carryin' the baby well. I checked a minute ago. He dropped down right good an' he seems to be turned right. It only be a matter of time 'til ya be a holdin' 'im in thet rockin' chair."

Marty couldn't hold back a groan at the next contraction, and Ma hurried into the room to soothe her and lay a cool cloth on her forehead. When Marty could catch her breath and relax some, she could see Clark, looking even whiter, sitting in a kitchen chair with his head bowed and lips moving. She knew he was praying for her and for the baby, and that was even more comforting than Ma's experienced hands.

Clark bundled Missie up and took her out to the barn with him so she might not hear the agonizing groans of her mama.

Marty held on, taking one contraction at a time, her face damp from the effort, her lips stifling the screams that wanted to come. Ma stayed close by, giving words of encouragement and administering what she could in advice and comfort.

Time ticked by so slowly—for Marty, who now marked time by contractions; for Clark, who, Ma told her, was trying with Missie's help to work on harnesses out in the barn; and for Ma herself, who obviously wanted the ordeal safely over for all of them.

The sun swung around to the west. Would this never end? wondered Marty between pains. It was agonizing. Ma kept telling her that from her years of experience, she knew the time was drawing near. Everything was in readiness. Then at a quarter to four, Marty gave a sharp cry that ended as a baby boy made his appearance into the world.

With a sob Marty lay back in the bed exhausted, so thankful that her work was done and that Ma's capable hands were there to do what was necessary for the new baby. A tired but joyful smile couldn't help but appear on Marty's face as she heard her son cry.

"He's jest fine," Ma said. "A fine, big boy."

In short order she had both baby and mother presentable and, placing the wee bundle on Marty's arm, went to bring the good news to Clark.

"He's here," Marty heard her call out the door, "an' he's a dandy."

Clark's running footsteps were clearly heard, and he soon came panting into the cabin, carrying Missie with him.

"She's okay?" His anxious eyes moved from Ma to the bedroom door as he set Missie down.

"Fit as a fiddle," Ma responded. Marty knew Ma was relieved, too. "She done a great job," Ma continued, "an' she's got a fine boy. Iffen ya slow down a mite an' take yerself in hand, I may even let ya git a small peek at 'im."

Clark took off his coat and unbundled Missie.

"Here, Missie, let's warm a bit afore we go to see yer mama," Marty heard him tell the little girl. They stood together at the fire, and then he lifted her up and followed Ma to the bedroom.

Clark stood by the bed and looked down at Marty. She was

tired, and she knew she probably didn't look her best after this long, difficult day, but she smiled up gallantly. His gaze shifted to the small bundle. Marty held the baby so Clark could see him better. He was a bit red yet, but he sure was one fine boy. One small clenched fist lay against his cheek.

"He's a real dandy," Clark said, the awe he was feeling showing in his tone. "What ya be a callin' 'im?"

"He be Claridge Luke," Marty answered.

"Thet's a fine name. What the Luke be for?"

"My pa."

"He'd be right proud could he see 'im. His pa'd be right proud, too, to have sech a fine son."

Marty nodded, a lump hurting her throat at the thought.

"Claridge Luke Davis." Clark said it slowly. "Right good-soundin' name. Bother ya any iffen I shorten it to Clare sometimes?"

"Not a'tall," said Marty. Indeed, she wondered if anything would ever bother her again.

They had both forgotten Missie during the exchange, and the little girl remained silent in her pa's arms, staring at the strange, squirming bundle. At last she inquired, as though trying to sort it out, "Ba-by?"

Clark's attention turned to her. "Yah, Missie, baby. That's the baby thet yer mama done got ya. Little Clare, he be."

"Rock . . . baby?" Missie asked.

"Oh no, not yet a while," laughed Clark. "First the baby an' yer mama have to have a nice long rest. We'd best be goin' now an' let them be."

Marty responded only with a slight smile. She was a strange

mixture of delirious happiness intermingled with sadness and was oh, so very tired.

I do declare, she thought as the two left the room, *I think thet be the hardest work I ever did in my whole lifetime,* and after slowly sipping some of Ma's special tea, she drifted off to sleep.

In the sitting room, Clark and Missie cuddled close in the rocking chair. "Missie, let's pray fer yer mama and the new baby." At her nod, he closed his eyes and prayed, "Thank ya, Father, thank ya for helping Ma, and fer Marty's safe birthin', an' thet fine new boy." His "amen" was echoed by the small girl in his lap.

Twenty-Two

Ma Bares Her Heart

Ma stayed on with Marty for several days after the arrival of little Claridge Luke.

"I wanna see ya back on yer feet like afore I leave ya be," Ma declared. "'Sides, there be nothin' pressin' at home jest now."

Marty was more than pleased to have the older woman's company and help. She was thrilled with her new son and eager to be up and around. Not being one who is happy when kept down, she was after Ma to let her get up from the second day on. Ma, reluctant at first, allowed her small activities that gradually grew with each day.

Missie, excited about the new baby, loved to share Marty's lap with him as they rocked in the chair. Clark seemed to take on a new air of family pride, declaring, "That little tyke has already growed half an inch and gained two pounds. I can see it by jest lookin'."

The day came when Marty felt sufficiently able to cope with managing the house and the children on her own. She was sure that even with Ma's kindness and generosity, she must be anxious to get home and look to her own.

Ma nodded her agreement. "Yeah, things do be goin' fine around here. Ya take care o' yerself an' things be jest right. I'll have Clark drive me on home tomorrow."

Marty would miss Ma when she left, but it would be good to have her little place all to herself again.

That afternoon as the two women had coffee together one more time, their conversation ranged over many topics. They talked of their families and their hopes for the future. Ma again expressed her need to adjust to Sally Anne's soon departure from the family nest.

"She seems so young yet," Ma said. "But ya know ya can't say no once a young'un has the notion."

"But she's not jest bein' a strong-willed girl," Marty countered. "She jest be in love. Don'cha remember, Ma, what it was like to be so young an' so in love thet yer heart missed beatin' at the sight o' him an' yer face flushed when ya wasn't wantin' it to? 'Member the wild feelin' thet love has?"

"Yeah, I reckon," Ma responded slowly. "Though 'twas so long ago. I do remember, though, when I met Thornton, guess I didn't behave myself much better than Sally Anne." Ma gave a short chuckle but quickly looked serious again.

"What was it like, Ma, when ya lost Thornton?"

"When I lost Thornton?" repeated Ma. "Well, it be a long time ago now. But I 'member it still, though it don't pain me sharp like it used to. Myself—way down deep—wanted to die, too; but I couldn't let that happen, me havin' three little ones to look out fer. I kept fightin' on, yet all the time I only felt part there. The rest of me seemed to be missin' or numb or somethin'."

"I know what ya mean," Marty said, her voice so low she wasn't sure she was heard. More loudly she said, "Then ya met Ben."

"Yeah, then I met Ben. I could see he be a good man an' one ya could count on."

"An' ya fell in love with 'im."

Ma paused, then shook her head. "No, Marty, there was no face flushin' an' fast heart skippin'."

Marty stared.

"No, it be different with Ben. I needed 'im, an' he needed me. I married 'im not fer love, Marty, but fer my young'uns—an' fer his."

Ma stopped talking and sat studying her coffee cup, turning it round and round in her hand. "Fact be, Marty—" She stopped again, and Marty knew this conversation was very difficult for her. "Fact be, at first I felt—well, guilty like. I felt like I be a . . . a loose woman, sleepin' with a man I didn't feel love fer."

If Ma hadn't seemed so serious, Marty would have found that statement humorous. It was hard to imagine Ma, a steady, solid, and plain woman, with a faith in God and a brood of eleven, as a "loose woman." But Marty did not laugh. She did not even smile. She understood some measure of the deep feelings being expressed by Ma Graham.

"I never knowed," Marty finally whispered. "I never woulda guessed thet ya didn't love Ben."

Ma's head came up in an instant, her eyes wide.

"Lan' sake, girl!" she exclaimed. "Thet were *then*. Why, I love my Ben now, ya can jest bet I do. Fact is, he's been a right good man to me, an' I 'spect I love 'im more'n I love myself."

"When—when an' how did it happen?" Marty asked, both

fascinated and a little frightened by what she might hear. "The head spinnin' an' the heart flutterin' an' all?"

Ma smiled. "No, there's never been thet. See . . . I learnt me a lesson. There's more than one way thet love comes. Oh, sure, sometimes it comes wild like, makin' creatures into wallerin' simpletons. I've seed 'em, I've been there myself; but it doesn't have to be thet way, an' it's no less real an' meanin'ful iffen it comes another way. Ya see, Marty, sometimes love comes sorta stealin' up on ya gradual like, not shoutin' bold words or wavin' bright flags. Ya ain't even aware it's a growin' an' growin' an' gettin' stronger until—I don't know. All the sudden it takes ya by surprise like, an' ya think, 'How long I been a feelin' like this an' why didn't I notice it afore?'"

Marty stirred. It was all so strange to get a peek inside of Ma like this. She pictured a young woman, widowed like herself, with pain and heartache doing what she had felt was best for her children. And Ma had felt . . . guilty. Marty shivered.

I do declare, she thought, *I couldn't have done it. Thanks be to whatever there be in charge of things thet I wasn't put in a position like thet. Me, I've jest had to be a mama.*

She pushed away from those thoughts and rose to get more coffee. She didn't want to even consider it anymore. Now Ma was happy again and she needn't feel guilty anymore. She now loved Ben. Just how or when it happened, she couldn't really say, but it had. It just—well, it just worked its way into her heart—slowly, softly.

Marty took a deep breath, pushed it all aside, and changed the subject.

Little Clare was getting round and dimpled, cooing at whoever would talk to him. Missie took great pride in her new baby "brudder." Clark was happy to take the "young fella" and rock him if he needed quieting or burping when Marty was busy getting a meal or cleaning up or doing the dishes. Marty was often tired by the end of the day, but she slept well, even though her nights were interrupted with feedings.

Clark was working doubly hard on the log cutting. He had told Marty that their cabin was too small, and come spring, he planned to tear off the lean-to and add a couple of bedrooms. Marty wondered if he had forgotten his promise of fare for her trip back home. Well, there was plenty of time to remind him of that. It was only the first of March.

Twenty-Three

Visitors

A new baby gave the neighbor ladies a delightful excuse to put aside their daily duties and go calling. So it was in the weeks following the arrival of little Clare that Marty welcomed some of her neighbors whom she had not previously known, except perhaps fleetingly as a face at Clem's funeral.

The first to come to see Marty and the baby was Wanda Marshall.

Marty set aside the butter she was churning and welcomed her sincerely. "So glad thet ya dropped by."

Small and young, with blond hair that at one time must have been very pretty, she had light blue eyes that somehow looked sad even as she smiled. Marty recognized her as the young woman who had spoken to her the day of Clem's funeral, inviting her to share their one-room home.

Wanda smiled shyly and presented a gift for the new baby.

When Marty opened the package, she found a small bib, carefully stitched and with embroidery so intricate she could scarcely understand how one could do such fine work. It looked delicate and dainty, like the giver, Marty thought. She thanked Wanda and exclaimed over the stitching, to which Wanda gave a slight shrug of her thin shoulders.

"I have nothing else to do."

"Lan' sake," said Marty, "seems I never find time fer nuthin' since young Clare came along. Even my evenin's don't give me much time fer jest relaxin'."

Wanda did not respond as her eyes gazed around the house. Eventually she spoke almost in a whisper. "Could I see the baby?"

"My, yes," Marty answered heartily. "He be havin' a sleep right now—he an' Missie—but iffen we tippy-toe in, we can have us a peek. Maybe we'll be able to have us coffee afore he wakes up wantin' his dinner."

Marty led the way into the bedroom. Wanda looked over at the sleeping Missie with her tousled curls and sleep-flushed cheeks. "She's a pretty child, isn't she?"

"Missie? Yeah, she be a dolly thet 'un," Marty said with feeling.

They then turned to Marty's bed, upon which little Clare was sleeping. He was bundled in the carefully made finery his proud mama had sewn for him. His dark head showed above the blanket, and stepping closer, one got a look at the soft pink baby face, with lashes as fine as dandelion silk on his cheeks. The small hands were free and one tiny fist held a corner of his blanket.

Marty couldn't help but think he looked beautiful, and she wondered that her visitor made no comment. When she looked up, it was to see her guest quickly leaving the bedroom.

Marty was mystified. Well, some folks you never could figure. She placed a tender kiss on Clare's soft head and followed Wanda Marshall back to the kitchen.

When Marty reached the kitchen, the young woman stood looking out of the window. Marty quietly went to add more wood to the fire and put on the coffee. Finally Wanda turned slowly and Marty saw with surprise that she had been struggling with tears.

"I'm sorry," she said with a weak attempt at a smile. "He's . . . he's a beautiful baby, just perfect."

She sat down at Marty's table, hands twisting nervously in her lap, her eyes downcast, seemingly to study the movement of her hands. When she looked up again, Marty thought she looked careworn and older than her years.

With another effort at a smile, she went on, "I'm sorry. I really am. I didn't know it would be so hard. I mean, I had no idea I'd react so foolishly. I'd . . . I'd love to have a baby. My own, you know. Well, I did. I mean—that is, I have had babies of my own. Three, in fact, but they've not lived—not any of them, two boys and one girl, and all of them . . ." Her voice trailed off; then her expression hardened. "It's this wretched country!" she burst out. "If I'd stayed back east where I belong, things would have been different. I would have my family—my Jodi and Esther and Josiah. It's this horrible place. Look . . . look what it did to you, too. Losing your husband and having to marry a . . . a stranger in order to survive. It's hateful, that's what—just hateful!"

By now the young woman was weeping in broken, heart-rending sobs. Marty stood rooted to the spot, holding slices of loaf cake. *Lan' sakes,* she thought frantically, *the poor thing. What do I do now?*

She took a deep breath for control and crossed to Wanda, laying a sympathetic hand on her shoulder. "I'm so sorry," she said softly. "So sorry. Why, iffen I'd lost young Clare, I don' know . . . I jest don' know iffen I could've stood it."

She made no further reference to her loss of Clem. This woman was battling with a sorrow Marty had not faced— bitterness. Marty continued. "I jest can't know how ya must feel, losin' three babies an' all, but I know ya must hurt somethin' awful."

By now Marty had her arms around the shaking shoulders and pulled the young woman against her. "It's hard, it's truly hard to be losin' somethin' thet ya want so much, but this I know, too—ya mustn't be blamin' the West fer it all. It could happen anywhere—anywhere. Womenfolk back east sometimes lose their young'uns, too. Ya mustn't hate this land. It's a beautiful land. An' you. Yer young an' have yer life ahead of ya. Ya mustn't let these tragedies bitter ya so. Don't do a lick o' good to be fightin' the way things be, when there be nuthin' a body can do to change 'em."

By now Wanda had been able to quiet her sobbing and seemed to allow herself the comfort of Marty's words and arms.

"Life be what ya make it, to be sure," Marty murmured. "No woman could find good in buryin' three of her babies, but like I said, you is young yet. Maybe"—she was about to say maybe Clark's God—"maybe the time thet lies ahead of ya will still give ya babies to hold an' love. Ya jest hold on an' keep havin' faith an' . . ."

Marty's voice trailed off. *Lan' sakes, I didn't know I could talk on so without stoppin'.*

"An' 'sides," Marty said as another thought overtook her, "we're gonna have a doc in town now, an' maybe with his help . . ."

She let the thought lie there with no further comment.

Wanda seemed at peace now. She lay against Marty for a few more minutes, then slowly straightened. "I'm sorry," she said. "I'm very foolish, I know. You're so kind and so brave, and you're right, too. I'll . . . I'll be fine. I'm glad . . . about the doctor."

The coffee was threatening to boil over, and Marty ran to rescue it. As they sat with their coffee and cake, Marty began their chat by asking Wanda about her background.

Marty learned that Wanda had been a "city girl," well bred, well educated, and perhaps a bit spoiled, as well. How she ever had gotten way out west still seemed a puzzle even to her. She shook her head as though she still couldn't quite fathom how it had all come about.

Clare fussed and Marty went to bring him out, nursing him as they continued their visit over coffee. Not knowing just what effect the baby's presence might have on Wanda, Marty kept him well hidden with the blanket.

Wanda talked on about having so little to do. She did beautiful stitching, that Marty knew, but she didn't have anyone to sew for. She didn't quilt, she couldn't knit or crochet, and she just hated to cook, so didn't do any more of that than she had to. She loved to read but had read her few books so many times she practically could recite them, and she had no way of getting more.

Marty offered the practical suggestion that she would teach her to quilt, knit, or crochet if she cared to learn.

"Oh, would you?" Wanda enthused. "I'd so much love to learn."

"Be glad to," Marty responded cheerily. "Anytime ya care to drop in, ya jest come right ahead."

Young Clare finished nursing and set himself to squirming.

Marty turned her attention to the baby, properly arranging her clothing and lifting him up for a noisy burp.

Wanda laughed quietly, then spoke softly. "Would you mind if I held him for a minute?"

"Not a'tall," Marty responded. "Why don't ya jest sit ya there in the rockin' chair a minute. He's already spoiled by rockin', I'm thinkin', so a little more won't make no difference."

Gingerly Wanda carried the baby to the rocking chair and settled herself with him snuggled up against her. Marty went to clear the table.

When Missie called a few minutes later and Marty crossed through the sitting room to get the little girl, she noticed Wanda gently rocking, eyes far away yet tender, baby Clare looking like he fully enjoyed the attention.

Poor thing, Marty's heart responded. *Poor thing. I be jest so lucky.*

Ma Graham came next, bringing with her a beautiful hand-knit baby shawl. Marty declared she'd never seen one so pretty. Ma brought her youngsters with her on this trip. They all were eager for their first look at their new little neighbor. Ma seemed to watch with thoughtful eyes as Sally Anne, eyes shining, held the wee baby close. Each one of Ma's children took a turn carefully holding the baby—even the boys, for they had been raised to consider babies as treasures indeed.

The group lunched together, and before it seemed possible, the afternoon was gone.

The next day an ill-clad stranger, with two equally ill-clad little girls, appeared at Marty's door. At Marty's welcoming "Won't ya come in," the woman made no answer but pushed a hastily wrapped little bundle at Marty.

Marty thanked her and unwrapped the gift to find another bib. Quite unlike the one that Wanda Marshall had brought—in fact, as different as it could be; the material was coarse, perhaps from a worn overall, though the stitches were neat and regular. There had been no attempt to fancy it up, and it looked rather wrinkled from handling. Marty, however, thanked the woman with simple sincerity and invited them once more to come in.

They came in shyly, all three with downcast eyes and shuffling feet.

"I don't remember meetin' ya afore," Marty ventured.

"I be . . ." the woman mumbled, still not looking up. Marty didn't catch if it was Rena or Tina or what it was, but she did make out Larson.

"Oh, ya be Mrs. Larson."

The woman nodded, still staring at the floor.

"An' yer two girls?"

The two referred to flushed deeply, looking as though they wished they could bury themselves in the folds of their mother's wrinkled skirt.

"This be Nandry an' this be Clae."

Marty wasn't sure she had heard it right but decided not to ask again.

As they waited for the coffee to boil, Marty took a deep breath and attempted to get the conversation going. "Be nice weather fer first of March."

The woman nodded.

"Yer man be cuttin' wood?"

She shook her head in the negative.

"He be a bit down," she finally responded, twisting her hands in her lap.

"Oh," Marty quickly grasped at this, hoping to find a connection with her withdrawn visitor. "I'm right sorry to be hearin' thet. What's he ailin' from?"

Mrs. Larson hunched a shoulder upward to indicate it was a mystery to her.

So be it fer thet, thought Marty sadly, picturing a husband and father driven to drink.

"Would ya like to see the baby?" she inquired.

The trio nodded.

Marty rose. "He be nappin' now. Come along."

She knew there was no need to caution for silence. This ghostly trio was incapable of anything louder than breathing, she was sure.

They reached the bed where the infant slept, and each one of the three raised her eyes from her worn shoes just long enough for a quick look at the baby. Was that a glimmer of interest in the younger girl's eyes? She probably imagined it, Marty decided, and she led the way back to the kitchen.

Marty was never more thankful to see a coffeepot boil in all of her life. Her visitors shyly helped themselves to a cookie when they were passed and seemed to dally over eating them as though to prolong the enjoyment. Marty got the feeling they didn't have cookies often. Marty wrapped up as many as she dared for them to take home. "We'll never be able to eat all these afore they get old," she assured the girls, carefully avoiding eye contact with their mother. She did not want to offend this poor woman.

They left as silently as they had come, watching the floor as they mumbled their good-byes.

Marty crossed to the kitchen window and watched them go.

They were walking. The drifts made the road difficult even for horses, and the air was cold with a wind blowing. She had noticed that none of her visitors were dressed very warmly. She watched as they trudged through the snow, leaning into the wind, clasping their too-flimsy garments about them, and tears formed in her eyes. She reached for the gift they had brought with them, and suddenly it became something to treasure.

Hildi Stern and Mrs. Watley came together. Hildi was a good-natured middle-aged lady. Not as wise as Ma Graham, Marty told herself, but a woman who would make a right fine neighbor.

Mrs. Watley—Marty didn't hear her given name—was a rather stout, boisterous lady. She didn't appear to be overly inclined to move about too much, and when Marty asked if they'd like to go to the bedroom for a peek at the baby, Mrs. Watley was quick with a suggestion. "Why don't ya jest bring 'im on out here, dear?"

They decided to wait until Clare finished his nap.

Each lady brought a parcel. Hildi Stern's gift was a small hand-knit sweater. Marty was thrilled with it.

Mrs. Watley presented her with another bib. This one, well sewn and as simple and unfussy as it could be, would be put to good use along with the others. Marty thanked them both with equal sincerity.

When they had finished their coffee, Mrs. Watley, looking like she enjoyed her several helpings of cookies and loaf cake, exclaimed what a grand little cook Marty was. Next they inspected the new baby. After they pronounced him a fine specimen, saying all of the things that a new mother expected to hear, Mrs. Watley turned to Hildi Stern.

"Why don't ya run along an' git the team, dear, an' I'll be a meetin' ya at the door?"

It was done.

Mrs. Vickers was the last of the neighbor visitors close enough that a new baby merited a drive on the winter roads. She had her boy, Shem, drive her over and sent him on to the barn with the horses while she came bustling up the walk, talking even before Marty got to the door to open it.

"My, my, some winter we be havin'. Though, I do declare, I see'd me worse—but I see'd me better, too—ya can jest count on thet—heerd ya had a new young'un—must be from the first mister, I says when I hears it—ain't been married to the other one long enough fer thet yet. How it be doin'? Hear he's a healthy 'un—an' thet's what counts, I al'ays say. Give me a healthy 'un any day over a purdy 'un—I al'ays say—take the healthy 'un ever'time."

She kicked the snow from her boots and came on into the kitchen. "My, my, ain't ya jest the lucky 'un—nice little place here. Sure beats thet covered wagon ya was livin' in. Not many women hereabout have a home nice as this, an' ya jest gettin' it all a handed to ya like. Well, let's see thet young'un."

Marty tactfully suggested they have coffee while Clare finished his nap, and Mrs. Vickers didn't turn the offer down. She settled herself on a kitchen chair and let her tongue slide over her lips as though adding oil to the machinery so it would run smoothly.

Marty had opportunity for little more than a slight nod of her head now and then. She thought maybe it was just as well. If she'd been given a chance for speech, she may have said some unwise things to her visitor.

Between Mrs. Vickers's helpings of loaf cake and gulps of coffee, Marty heard that:

"Jedd Larson be nothin' but one lazy good-fer-nothin', al'ays gettin' started when ever'one else be done—'ceptin' when it come to eatin' or drinkin' or raisin' young'uns—they been married fer ten years—already had 'em eight young'uns—only three thet lived, though—buried five—his missus—so ashamed an' mousy like—wouldn't no one 'round even bother to go near—"

Marty made herself a promise that come nice weather she'd pay a call on Mrs. Larson.

"Thet Graham clan—did ya ever see so many kids in the self-same family? Almost an insult to humans, thet's what it be—bad as cats or mice—havin' a whole litter like thet—"

Marty found herself hard put to hold her tongue.

"See'd thet young Miz Marshall yet? I declare me—thet young prissy woulda been better off to stay her back east where she be belongin'—her an' her first-class airs—an' not even able to raise her a young'un—woman's got no business bein' out west if she can't raise a young'un—an' confident like—I think there be somethin' funny there—hard to put yer finger on—but there all the same—doesn't even give ya a proper welcome when ya call—me, I called, neighbor like, when each of the young'uns died—told her right out what she prob'ly be a doin' wrong— well, ya know what—she most turned her back on me—"

Poor Wanda, thought Marty, aching once more for her new friend.

"Well, now—if that's the way she be, I says, leave her to it. Have Hildi and Maude been over? I see'd 'em go by t'other day— goin' over to see thet new young'un of the Davises, I says to myself—well, Hildi be a fine neighbor—though she do have some strange quirks—me, I'm not one to be a mentioning 'em. Maude Watley, now—thet be another matter—wouldn't do nothin' thet took any effort, thet one—she wasn't always big as the West itself—be there a time afore she catched her man thet she be a dance-hall girl—she wouldn't want one knowin' it o' course—but it be so—have ya been to town yet?"

At Marty's shake of her head, she hurried ahead.

"Well, mind ya, when ya do go, don't ya be tellin' nuthin' to thet there Miz McDonald thet ya don't want spread 'round thin like. She be a first-rate tongue wagger, thet 'un."

Marty also found out that Miz Standen, over to town, had her a Saturday beau.

"I'm bettin' thet the visitin' parson had him somethin' to hide, or he'd settle himself to one place." The woman dropped her voice as if someone else might hear the dark secret.

"The Krafts are expectin' them another young'un—makin' five."

"Milt Conners, the bachelor of the area, seems to be gettin' stranger ever'day. Should git 'im a woman—thet would be doin' him some good—he's gettin' liquor somewhere, too—nobody knows where, but I do have my s'picions."

And on and on she went, like a walking newspaper. The new doc would be arriving in April—folks saying Clark bought him— well, they needed a doc—hope he was worth it and not here just to make money on people's woes.

Young Sally Anne was hitching up with Jason Stern— supposed those two families be pairing off regular like in the next few years.

The woman finally stopped for a breath, and Marty wondered aloud that Shem had not come in from the barn and supposed he was getting cold and tired of waiting. Well, she'd send a slice of cake and a gingerbread cookie or two out with Mrs. Vickers.

Mrs. Vickers must have taken the hint and made her way out the door, still chattering as she left. Marty's head was spinning and her ears tingling. The visitor hadn't even looked at the baby.

Twenty-Four

New Discoveries

The days of March were busy ones for Clark. Marty watched as he pushed himself hard at the logging, working as long as there was light and then doing the chores with the aid of the lantern. Each night at the supper table he tallied up the total logs he'd felled for the new addition, and together they kept track of how many more were needed.

Marty's days were full, too, doing the usual housework and caring for the new baby and Missie. With the increased laundry needs, she found it difficult to get the clothes dry between one washing and the next.

In the evenings after the children were down for the night, both Clark and Marty were happy to sit quietly before the open fire, Marty with her quilt pieces or knitting, Clark with one of his books, working on some project, or mending some small tool of one kind or another. Marty found it increasingly comfortable to talk with Clark. In fact, she looked forward to relating the events of the day and reporting on Missie's conversations with her.

Clark had spent many evenings fashioning a new bed for Missie so the fast-growing Clare would be able to take over the crib. Marty enjoyed watching the bed take shape. She noticed the few simple tools Clark worked with responded well to his capable hands. She carefully pieced the quilt that would go on the bed and felt a growing sense of a shared accomplishment.

As they worked, they talked about the people and happenings that made up their little world. The early fall and long winter had brought animals down from the hills in search of food. Lately a couple of coyotes had been moving in closer and closer at nights, and Clark and Marty chuckled together about poor Ole Bob's noisy concern at the intrusion.

The neighbors were rarely seen during the winter months, so news was scarce. Clark said measles had been reported in town, but no serious cases had developed.

The two talked of spring planting and plans for the new bedroom, hoping that spring would be early rather than late in coming. They laughed about Missie's attempts at mothering her "brudder Clare." It wasn't any particular conversation or subject, but they probably were discovering deeper things about each other without actually being aware of the fact. Feelings, dreams, hopes, and, yes, faith were shared in a relaxed, ordinary way.

One evening as Marty quilted and Clark sanded the headboard for the bed, their talk turned to the Scripture passage he had read aloud at breakfast that morning. Having no background in such things, Marty found that a lot of the truths she heard from the Bible were difficult to understand. Over time

Clark had explained about the promises to the Jewish people of a Messiah who would come. But their perception of His purpose in coming was far different from what He actually came to accomplish. They wanted freedom from their oppressors; He came to give freedom from self and sin. They wanted to be part of a great earthly kingdom, but His kingdom was a heavenly one.

Marty was beginning to understand some of the things concerning the Messiah, but there were still a lot of unanswered questions in her mind.

"Do ya really think thet God, who runs the whole world like, be knowin' you?" she asked forthrightly.

"I'm right sure thet He do," Clark responded simply.

"An' how can ya be so sure?"

Clark looked thoughtfully at the Book carefully placed on the shelf near the table. "I believe the Bible, and it tells me thet He does. And because He answers my prayers."

"Ya mean by givin' ya whatever ya ask fer?"

Clark thought a minute, then shook his head. "No, not thet. Oft times He jest helps me to git by without what I asked fer."

Marty shook her head. "Thet seems ta be a strange idea."

Clark looked at her a moment, then said, "I'm thinkin' not so strange. A lot of times, what folks ask fer, they don't need a'tall."

"Like what?"

"Like good crops, new plows, an extry cow or two."

"What about iffen ya lose something thet ya already had an' had sorta set yer mind on?"

He didn't hesitate. "Ya mean like Clem or Ellen?"

Marty nodded slowly.

"He don't take away the hurt, but He sure do share it with ya."

"Wisht I woulda had me someone to share mine with."

"He was there, an' I'm thinkin' thet He helped ya more than ya was aware."

"But I didn't really know to ask Him to."

"I did."

Twenty-Five

Catastrophe!

On March sixteen little Clare marked his first month in the family. So far he had been a first-rate baby, but Clark kept warning, "Jest ya wait 'til he starts cuttin' his teeth."

Marty told Clark she hoped he would be wrong—and Clark fervently hoped so, too. "Missie had herself a plumb awful time with them teeth," he told her.

The day had turned colder again after some hints of spring, and it looked like another storm might be hitting soon. Clark had left early in the morning to restock their supplies.

He was back earlier than usual, and the anticipated storm was still holding off. Mrs. McDonald had sent a small parcel for the baby. Marty opened it and found another small bib.

"I do declare," she laughed. "Thet boy sure be well set up fer bibs. Guess he be well fixed fer droolin' when those teeth come in."

Clark laughed with her.

Missie's bed had been completed by now and set up in the

bedroom, and the small crib was moved into the sitting room, where it was warmer for the baby during the day. He was awake more often now and liked to lie and look around, waving his small fists frantically in the air. Marty still took him into the bed with her at night.

When the day ended and evening fell, Clark and Marty both noticed a shift in the wind. Clark commented, "Guess we not be gettin' thet storm tonight after all."

The thought was a welcome one. Large drifts of snow still lay over the ground, and their hopes for an early spring were disappointed regularly. The weather mostly stayed cold with occasional snow flurries, and the arctic winds made winter's long stay even drearier.

With Clark's hurried trip to town and Marty having baked bread as well as done the washing for the baby, they were both tired from a long day's work, so Clark said good-night and headed for the lean-to.

Marty tucked herself in, stretching her toes deep into the warm blankets. She nursed young Clare so he would sleep as far into the night as possible and settled down with him tucked in beside her. She thought she had barely fallen asleep when she was awakened with Clark bending over her, hurriedly pulling on his jacket.

"The barn be ablaze. Ya jest stay put. I'm goin' fer the stock," and he was gone.

Marty's head felt foggy with sleep. Had she had a dream? No, she was sure he really had been there. What should she do? It seemed to take forever before she finally was able to move, though in truth it no doubt was a matter of seconds. She scrambled from the bed, making sure Clare and Missie were both sleeping, and then, without stopping to dress herself or even slip into her house socks, she ran through the house to the kitchen window. Before she even pulled the curtain aside she could see the angry red glow. Horror filled her as she looked at the scene. The barn's roof was on fire, with leaping flames towering into the dark sky and smoke pouring upward, and there was Clark silhouetted against the frightening scene. He had swung open the barn door and smoke was billowing out.

As Marty realized what he had actually said to her and saw him about to enter the inferno, her own voice choked out, sounding as desperate in her ears as she felt, "No, Clark, no. Don't go in there, please, please—"

But he had gone—for the animals. *We can get more animals, Clark,* her heart silently cried.

Marty stood at the window—watching, straining, dying a thousand deaths in what seemed forever, praying as best she could. And then through the smoke plunged Charlie—or was it Dan?—and right behind him came the other horse, rearing and pawing the air. The saddle horse came close behind, dragging his halter rope and tossing his head wildly. He ran until he crashed stupidly into the corral fence, falling back only to struggle up again to race around frantically.

Marty stared unblinking at the barn door. "Oh, Clark, Clark, please, please. God, iffen ya can hear me, please let 'im come out," she whispered through teeth clenched tightly together.

But the next dark shape to come through the smoke was a milk cow, then another, and another.

"Oh, God!" sobbed Marty. "He'll never make it."

The walls of the barn were now engulfed in flame, too. The

fire licked hungrily along the wall, reaching terrifying fingers toward the open door. And then she saw him, stumbling through the entrance, dragging harnesses with him and staggering along until he reached the corral fence. She could see him clinging to it for support and pulling a wet towel he must have grabbed on his way out away from his head and face.

"Oh, God!" cried Marty as she collapsed in a heap on the cold kitchen floor.

Somehow the long night blurred together from then on. Marty simply couldn't take it all in. Clark was safe, but the barn was gone. Neighbor men, with water and snow, seemed to be everywhere, now fighting to save the other outbuildings.

Women were there, too, bustling about her, talking, giving the men a hand by turns, making up sandwiches and coffee. Marty felt numb with emotional exhaustion. Someone placed baby Clare in her arms.

"He's cryin' to eat," she said. "Best ya sit ya down an' nurse 'im."

She did. That much she could understand.

When morning came, the barn lay in smoldering ruins, but the sheds had been saved.

Tired, smoky faces gathered around a hastily made campfire in the yard for the coffee and sandwiches. Their clothes and boots were ice crusted, and their hands cupped around mugs for warmth. They talked in hushed tones. Losing one's barn and feed, with winter still in full swing, was a great loss, and each one knew it only too well.

Eventually the men quietly gathered their women, anxious to be home and out of frozen clothing. Just as the first team left the yard, Jedd Larson arrived with his team.

"Good ole Jedd." Marty heard an annoyed whisper. "Prob'ly be late fer his own buryin'."

Jedd took over where the others had left off, helping himself to a cup of coffee and grabbing up a sandwich. As the neighbor families, one by one, took their leave, he appeared to be settling in for a long chat.

Poor Clark, Marty thought as she glanced anxiously out the kitchen window. *He jest be lookin' beat. All ashes an' soot an' half frozen, an' now Jedd wants to sit an' jaw him to death—no sense a'tall, thet Jedd. Well, I won't 'low it,* and pulling her shawl about her shoulders, she marched out.

"Mr. Larson," she greeted the man, keeping her voice even. "Right good of ya to be comin' over to give us a hand. Guess things be under control like now, thanks to all our fine neighbors. Have ya had coffee? Good! I'm sorry to be interruptin' like, but right now I'm afeared thet my husband be needed indoors—iffen ya can be excusin' 'im."

She had never referred to Clark as her husband before, and Clark's cup paused midway to his mouth, but he said nothing. She gave a meaningful nod toward the door, and Clark added his thanks to Jedd and went into the house.

"Give yer missus our greetin's," Marty told the man. "We won't be keepin' ya any longer, ya havin' chores at home waitin' on ya an' all. Ya'll be welcome to come agin when ya can sit an' chat a spell. Bring yer family along. Thank ya agin. One really 'preciates fine neighbors. I'd best be gettin' in to my young'uns. Good day, Mr. Larson."

Marty turned to the house, looking over her shoulder as Jedd Larson crawled into his wagon and aimed it for home. She noticed he didn't have the wagon box moved to the sleigh runners yet. No doubt he had kept planning on getting to it but just hadn't found the time.

Marty entered the house to find a puzzled Clark. "I was thinkin' Missie would be in some kind o' state and would need some comfortin' from her pa, but she's still sleepin' sound like," he said. "Clare's awake, but he don't look none the worse for wear." Clark grinned down at the contented baby in the crib. "Who be needin' me?" he asked wryly.

She stared at him dumbly, seeing his lips were cracked and bleeding from the heat of the fire. She had bravely, if nearly frantic with worry, held on through the night, answering questions about where to find the coffee and all and was she okay. She had restrained herself from running out into the barnyard to see if Clark was really all right. She had kept herself from angrily lashing out against whoever or whatever had let such a disastrous thing happen to Clark, he who worked so hard, who helped his neighbors, who was so patient and talked quietly and never lost his temper, who didn't drink and mistreat his family, who believed in God and prayed to Him daily, who lived by the Book and what it said.

Why, why did this have to happen to Clark? she railed silently. *Why not lazy Jedd Larson or—or . . .* After having lived through this tragic night, and now seeing Clark safe in front of her, Marty could hold it all in no longer. She turned away, leaned against the wall, and let the sobs overtake her.

She felt his hands on her shoulders, and he turned her to him, then pulled her gently into his arms. He held her close like he would a weeping child, stroking the long hair falling over her shoulders. He said nothing and simply let her weep against his chest.

Finally she was able to stop, all the confusion and anger drained from her. She pulled herself away, wiping her face on her apron. "Oh, Clark," she whispered, "whatever air we gonna do now?"

He didn't answer for a moment, and then he spoke so calmly she knew he felt sure of his answer. "Well, we're gonna pray, an' what He sees us to be needin', He'll give; an' what He sees we don' need, He'll make us able to do without."

Marty led the way to the table, and they sat and bowed their heads together. Then Clark reached for the Book, quietly opened it, and began reading, "'The Lord is my shepherd; I shall not want. . . .'"

When Clark came in for breakfast after chores that morning, Marty learned that the cows had run off in terror. The horses, too, had scattered. The pigs were safe in their pens, as were the chickens, but Clark was hard put finding enough to satisfy them without delving too deeply into the precious seed grain that had escaped the blaze. The grazing stock, one pasture over, stood in their shelter bawling to be fed, but with what? All their feed had gone up in smoke. "I jest did the best thet I could fer now," Clark commented with a shrug.

Marty fretted over his cracked lips and blistered hands, but Clark lightly brushed aside her concern.

Missie was strangely quiet as they ate, no doubt sensing something was amiss as she looked between her pa and mama.

Finally Marty could hold the question in no longer. "What ya plannin' to do?"

"First off, I'm goin' over to Ben's," Clark answered matter-of-factly. "He said he'd be right glad to take two of the milk cows. He'll feed 'em both in exchange fer the milk from the one thet's still milkin'. When I have me feed again, we'll get 'em back."

"An' the rest of the stock?"

"We'll have to be sellin' the fifteen head in the grazin' pen."

"An' the hogs?"

"Most of 'em will have to go. I hope to spare me a young sow or two."

"How ya be feedin' 'em?"

"The seed grain wasn't lost. It's in the bins by the pig lot. I'll have to hold me off plantin' thet new land I'd been countin' on 'til another year an' use some of the grain to feed a sow through to spring."

"An' the horses?"

"Horses are fair good at grazin' even in the winter. They can paw down through the snow. I'll take me a bit of money from the sellin' of the stock to git me enough feed to look to the one milk cow thet we keep."

"Ya got it all figured already," Marty said in awe.

"Not quite all, but I been workin' on it. We maybe have to skimp a bit here an' there, but we'll make it. Iffen all goes well, come crop time, we'll be gettin' on our feet agin."

An' the fare back east? Marty didn't ask the question out loud, but Clark somehow must have seen the question in her eyes.

He looked steadily at her for a moment, then spoke slowly. "When I asked ya to set yerself in here to care fer Missie, I made a promise to ya. I'm not goin' back on it now. To tell ya the truth, I would be a missin' ya should ya go, you an' the young'uns"—he stopped and Marty could see his Adam's apple

193

move as he swallowed—"but I'll not be a holdin' ya iffen it's what ya be a wantin'."

For the first time, Marty was no longer sure.

Clark carried through his plans for the stock. The hogs, except for two promising young sows, were sold, as was the grazing stock. He decided to buy enough feed for the milk cow and the two sows and to save the seed grain so the new field could be sown after all. They would need the money from the crop more than ever to help with expenses until the livestock built up again. Only a few hens were saved. The rest were put in crates and taken to town.

Clark now was faced with even more logs to cut since, come spring, a new barn would have to be built.

"Don't worry none about the extry room," Marty told him. "We'll need the barn first." But he said he thought he could manage both with only a slight delay on the house.

The corral fence was repaired, and the single cow and team of horses were placed in the grazing pen, where there was shelter for them. The saddle horse was lent to Jason Stern, who seemed to have great need of it for the present.

Somehow life fell into a routine again. No one was wishing for spring more fervently than Marty, but she found herself wanting it for Clark more than for herself.

Twenty-Six

Barn Raisin'

March blew itself out in an angry snarl of wind and snow; then April's arrival promised better things. As the month progressed, the snow began to melt into lacy crystals, the sun took on new warmth, and patches of green gradually appeared in sheltered places. Dan and Charlie greedily sought out each bit of green, eager for easier feeding after foraging through the snow since the fire. The Guernsey had ceased giving milk, readying herself for calving. Milk for Missie and for cooking now had to be brought by pail from the Grahams' every few days.

Near the end of the month, Marty looked out at the nearly bare garden. How eager she was to get at its planting. Cooped up all these months, she could hardly wait to get to some tasks that could be done out-of-doors.

However, Clark had other things that must be done before getting the ground ready for Marty's garden. Over the last month, the neighbor men had brought their teams and given Clark a hand with the logging. Now the logs were stacked and ready for the raising of the new barn. If they had a good day, they'd even give a hand with the two new bedrooms, they promised.

Marty looked out now, envisioning the new barn standing where the old one had been. How good it would be for Clark—and the animals—to have a barn again. The bedrooms—she'd wait on them as long as she had to.

But the first big event for the community was to be the house raising for young Jason Stern and Sally Anne Graham, a house being even more important for the two than a barn. Tomorrow was set aside for the "raisin'," and Marty had been busy draining kraut, cooking ham, and baking extra bread and pie. The men would offer their labors, and the womenfolk would open their larders. Marty looked forward to the day. It would be so welcome to have a visit with her neighbors.

The house raising went well, and the men finished the task in the late afternoon. The women enjoyed a day chatting about their families and sharing recipes and patterns. The Larsons were late, and when they did arrive, Mrs. Larson timidly set her pot of potato stew on the table laden with good things. For the most part no one seemed to pay her much mind, but Marty crossed over to at least say a "howdy" and a welcome to the obviously lonely woman.

Her husband, Jedd, was there to give a hand only on the last few logs, then seemed to consider his advice of far more worth than his brawn. He did, however, manage to down a hearty meal along with the rest.

Marty went home contented with the outing and what was accomplished. Sally Anne would have a nice little cabin in which to set up her first housekeeping. True, there was still a lot that needed to be done, but Marty was sure that Jason would soon take care of that.

During the day, Marty had had a nice long visit with Wanda Marshall, showing her a simple crochet pattern and finding her a keen student of the handwork.

Mrs. Vickers had buzzed about, whispering choice bits of news in various ears, and Mrs. Watley had planted herself in a sunny spot by the desserts and busied herself with drinking coffee and "keepin' the young'uns outen the food."

It was all fun, Marty decided, and next week would be their turn to host the neighbors and be the recipients of their cheerful efforts.

True to their word, the group started arriving on Tuesday morning, determined to get the job done. Log by log the barn began to take shape. Clark and Todd Stern manned the axes that skillfully cut the grooves so one log might fit the next. Clark had decided to build the barn a mite larger to accommodate the animals he anticipated in the future.

By the time the women banged the pot to announce dinner, the barn had nearly reached the rafter stage. The men were eager to get back to their work, so did not tarry long over their meal.

While the women were doing up the dishes, Tommy Graham came in and casually announced, "Pa said iffen ya be movin' the things from the lean-to, we be tearin' it off an' makin' the bedrooms."

Marty fairly flew. She had never been in the lean-to before and was rather shocked at its spartan furnishings. The bedframe held a coarse straw tick. Marty laid her hand on it and thought it hard and lumpy. Remembering her own soft feather tick gave her a bit of a pang. *It must've been awfully cold out here all winter,* she thought guiltily as she moved the few articles Clark had into the sitting room, as well as his clothes from the pegs.

Marty was scarcely finished when she heard the hammers and crowbars have at it. The men went to work with a will, and by supper the logs were in place.

Supper was almost festive. The men were well pleased—and rightly so—with all that had been completed in just one day. Marty could tell that Clark Davis was a favorite neighbor. There wasn't a man there he hadn't helped out at one time or another, and it pleased them to be able to lend a hand in return.

When the meal was over, the men visited while the women cleaned up the tables and sorted out their own crockery and pans for the return to their homes.

Jedd had set a new record for himself on that day. He had made it in time for both dinner and supper, partaking freely of both meals. His missus couldn't make it. "Feelin' poorly," he said. Marty felt genuinely sorry for the poor woman and their daughters.

At last the group had all said their good-byes and clambered into their various farm wagons and onto horses, some promising to be back to help with the roof and floors.

Clark was almost half dead on his feet, having attempted to carry more than his share of the load at his own "raisin'" and then having to go out for choring after it was all over. He stretched out on the straw tick now lying on the sitting room floor, announcing he meant to just rest a bit before he went to bed "proper like" in the new addition. In next to no time he was sound asleep, snoring softly while Marty put the children to bed.

Marty came into the room and stopped short. "Lan' sakes," she exclaimed softly, "he be plumb beat."

She went over to gently ease a pillow under his head and slip off his shoes, then placed a blanket over him and moved in to her own bed.

Twenty-Seven

Laura

In less than two weeks' time the visiting preacher would be paying his spring visit, and Sally Anne would be marrying. Ma still mourned to think of her oldest moving out of the family circle, but she told Marty she guessed it was a part of life, and from now on she'd be losing them one by one.

But second daughter Laura's strange behavior troubled her mother. The girl had been acting so different lately, sullen and resentful around the house, then slipping away for long walks. At times she even rode off on one of the workhorses.

Marty didn't find all this out till some time after the fact, but finally Ma could take it no longer and knew she must have a talk with the girl. She waited for a time when they were alone, then began as gently as she could.

"Laura, I be thinkin' thet somethin's troublin' ya. I'd be right glad to be a sharin' it iffen ya'd like to lay it on me."

Laura seemed to look at Ma with rebellion in her eyes.

"Nothin' the matter with me," she responded resentfully.

"I think there is. Maybe it's a natural thing—with all the fussin' an' fixin' fer Sally Anne."

Laura's chin went up. "What do I care 'bout Sally Anne?"

"She be yer sister—"

"No, she ain't."

Ma looked fully at the girl now. Anger began to stir within her.

"Ya listen here, missy. Sally an' you been close like ever since I be yer ma."

"Ya ain't my ma."

Ma stopped short, and she told Marty later that she was sure her mouth was hanging open. She had known things were bad but had not guessed they were this bad. Finally she started over slowly. "Laura, I'm sorry, really I am. I never knowed ya was feelin' this way—so strong like. I've tried to be a ma to ya. I love ya like ya was my own, and yer pa—he'd do most anythin' fer ya."

"Won't need to be a doin' fer me much longer now," declared Laura.

"Whatcha meanin'?"

"I'm gettin' married, too."

"Yer gettin' married? But ya ain't even had ya a beau."

"Have too."

"Well, we never knowed it. Who be—?"

"Milt Conners." Laura stared back with stubborn determination in her face, no doubt well aware of the Grahams' view of the young man in question.

Ma reeled inwardly, turmoil and consternation making her nearly weak with the announcement from Laura. Never in her life would she give one of her daughters to Milt Conners. Not if her life depended on it. His drinking and carousing were well known in these parts, and not just hearsay.

When finally she could speak again, she tried her best to be firm yet gentle. "Oh no, ya ain't," she began. "No one in this house be takin' themselves up with Milt Conners. Iffen I didn't stop ya, yer pa sure would."

"Ya can't stop me!" Laura's assertion seemed to shock her as much as Ma. The girl took a tentative step backward.

"Oh yes'm, we can," said Ma, equally determined.

"It be too late," flung out Laura.

"Whatcha be meanin'?"

"I'm . . . I'm gonna have his baby." Now Laura's eyes were downcast, and she wouldn't look Ma in the face.

Ma told Marty she felt a weakness go all through her and thought she'd have a faint. Finally she staggered forward and steadied herself on the back of a chair. "Whatcha be sayin', girl?" she managed to ask.

But Laura stood her ground. Let Ma and Pa fume and fuss or anything else. Come time for Sally Anne to be standing before the preacher, she'd be there, too.

"I'm gonna have his baby," she repeated, more firmly this time.

Ma stepped forward, tears streaming down her face. She reached out for Laura and pulled her gently into her arms, holding her close, her head bowed against the long brown hair.

"Oh, my poor baby," she wept. "My poor, poor baby."

Ma's genuine love and care seemed to touch Laura, but the girl stoutly insisted that she loved Milt and was going to marry him come what may.

The two weeks until the preacher's visit were full of wedding preparations as well as deep sorrow in the Graham home. When Sally Anne heard of Laura's planned wedding, she generously offered to share some of her own household articles she had been stitching and preparing. Laura would have none of them, declaring she wouldn't need much, as Milt was already set up for housekeeping. Nevertheless, Ma sat up late each night, making a quilt and hemming towels and curtains.

Ben carried on with his usual farm work, but his shoulders sagged, and his face appeared drawn. The joy of the big day had been stolen from them. Even Laura did not seem to carry the glow that a new bride should, but she set her jaw determinedly and helped in preparations for the double wedding.

Twenty-Eight

The Big Day

The preacher's visit would occur on Easter Sunday morning. The community would first have an outdoor service together, then the wedding ceremonies would follow. Later the neighbors would all join for a potluck dinner to honor the new couples and to have a chance for a neighborly visit before spring work would demand much of their time.

Marty looked forward to the day. She was very grateful for the neighbors she had come to know and the friends she had made. With winter behind them and the feeling of spring in the air, she was restless to get out somewhere—for something. She also was curious about the church service and what the preacher would have to say. Her only connection with church had been for marriages and funerals, and the last time she had seen this preacher, she had been in such grief and emotional turmoil she could hardly remember the event or him.

She felt happiness for Sally Anne with the sparkle of love on her face, but her heart ached for Laura. After Ma had confided the reason for their consent to the marriage, Marty shared Ma's deep concern over the coming union and felt such helplessness, knowing there was nothing any of them could do to prevent further heartache for this strong-willed girl or her family.

Marty busied herself embroidering two sets of pillowcases for the new brides. She was fearful lest her true feelings show themselves even in her stitching. The one pair was so much joy to work. The other made her fingers feel as heavy as her heart.

Soon enough the big day arrived. The sun promised a warm spring day as Marty bustled about readying the pots of food that she would be taking and getting Missie and Clare dressed in their finest.

She decided she would wear her as yet unworn blue-gray dress. She finally accepted that she would "feel right" in it. Clark did look at her with admiration, and she found she didn't mind it. She felt herself flush under his gaze.

Marty's eyes cast joyfully about the yard and the surrounding hills as they packed up the wagon. A child at her side and babe in arms, she faced the bright morning beside Clark, pointing out each new sign of spring. Though the fields were now bare, with only patches of soiled snow left in hidden places, the first flowers were slowly lifting their heads to the sun. Returning birds occasionally made an appearance on a fence post or tree limb. But the surest sign of spring was the feeling within her as she breathed in the warm, fragrant air.

They were one of the first families to reach the Grahams', and Marty wanted to help Ma with the last of the preparations. Clark assured her that Missie and Clare would be fine left with him; the fresh air would do them all good. As Marty turned to hurry into the house, she heard Ben's comments on what a fine-looking son Clare was and Clark's gentle boasts of the tiny boy's already apparent strength and awareness. Marty smiled to herself.

Makeshift benches had been placed around for the church service, and long tables were arranged for the meal.

Ma's house was soon a hive of activity, for a visit from the preacher and two weddings on the same day were cause for any amount of flurry.

The Stern family arrived, causing Sally Anne to flush a becoming shade. Marty was glad to see Jason look at her with pride and love in his eyes.

Just before the service was to begin, Milt Conners appeared, looking as cocky and troublesome as ever. The men sociably made room for him on the bench, but Marty could understand the distress of the Grahams. She could not feel at ease about this man, either.

After all were seated on the benches, Ben Graham stood to his feet and welcomed the neighbors to his farm on this "fine spring day." He trusted they would find the Easter service a "real blessin'" and invited them to share in the weddings of his two eldest daughters, thanking them kindly "fer all the good food appearin' on the tables."

He then introduced the visiting preacher, Pastor Simmons, and expressed how "fine it is to have 'im here on Easter Sunday mornin', an' I know we's all lookin' forward to sharin' in the mornin' meetin'."

The pastor took charge of things then, and he commented on the "beautiful day that the Lord hath made," expressed his delight at seeing them all in attendance, and led the group in prayer. They sang a few hymns from memory, not having any hymnals. Marty didn't know the words to any of the hymns, but she enjoyed listening to the others sing. She must get Clark to teach her some of the tunes and words to the songs, she decided.

When Pastor Simmons began to speak to the people, Marty listened intently. The simple but powerful story of Easter began with Christ's ministry to the people of His day, His arrest, and the false accusations that sentenced Him to die. The preacher told of the political factions of the time and the historical reasons for His death, but he then explained the real purpose in the Father allowing, yea, planning for His beloved Son to die.

Marty's heart was torn as she listened. She had heard before how cruel men of Christ's day had put Him to death with no just cause, but never before had she realized it had anything at all to do with her. Now to hear the fact that He personally took the punishment for her sins, as well as for the sins of all mankind, was a startling and sobering discovery.

I didn't know—I jest didn't know thet ya died fer me, her heart cried as she sat on one of the benches, Clare held tightly in her arms and Missie and Clark on either side. *I'm sorry—truly I am. Lord, I asks ya to be doin' what yer intendin' in my heart.* Tears slipped from her eyes and down her cheeks. She didn't even bother to wipe them away. She could feel Clark's eyes on her when he occasionally glanced her way.

But the preacher did not stop there. He went on with the story of that first Easter morning when the women went early to the tomb and found the Lord had risen.

"He lives," said the preacher, "and because He is victor over sin and death, we, too, can be."

Marty's heart filled with such a surge of joy she felt like shouting—but not here, not now, she cautioned herself. She would eventually, though. She had to tell someone that now she understood. *I've given myself to be a knowin' Clark's God,* she told herself, awed by the thought.

She reached over and slipped her hand into Clark's. When Clark looked at her, she returned his gaze. He must have read the difference in her face, and the big hand firmly squeezed her smaller one. Marty knew he shared her joy, as she now shared his God. It was enough.

The weddings followed the worship service. Laura and Milt stood together first in front of the pastor. Sally Anne had wanted it that way. Milt looked down at his feet, shifting back and forth with regularity. He looked rather careless in demeanor and attire, though he had trimmed his beard and had a haircut. Laura looked shyly at him in a way that made Marty hope maybe, with the help of a good woman's love, this man could indeed change. She wanted with all her heart for the two of them to find happiness together.

Jason and Sally Anne stood next, and Marty knew the joy and love showing on their faces was reflected in the Grahams' as well as her own heart. How easy it was to share in their happiness.

As soon as the ceremonies were over, the neighbors began the merrymaking, throwing rice, ringing cowbells, and lining up to kiss the brides. The two couples were finally allowed to sit down at the table piled with gifts, and while the womenfolk made preparations for the noon meal, the brides unwrapped their presents.

As the good-natured talk and laughter continued during the meal, the Larsons arrived. Jedd swaggered over to the tables, not even bothering to tether his team. Mrs. Larson placed a pan of corn bread with the other dishes and, with eyes to the ground, ushered her youngsters to a safe-looking place at a far table. Marty rose and, with a pretense of refilling the water pitcher, passed close to the woman.

"Ya all be welcome. So glad ta see ya agin'," Marty said softly. The woman did not lift her eyes, but a small spot of color appeared in each cheek as she nodded in answer. "The good Lord has done so much fer all of us," Marty continued, reaching out to tousle each child's hair. "Preacher talked 'bout it this mornin', how God can clean up folks' hearts and change their ways. He's put me on that path," she added, not exactly sure how to express what she was feeling.

Marty's feelings soared with satisfaction as she noticed Mrs. Larson's upward glance. Wasn't that an expression of hope? Meanwhile, Jedd just loaded his plate and settled down to eat. Further visiting with Mrs. Larson could come at another time.

When the tables had been cleared away, the two new young couples loaded their wagons and kissed Ma good-bye. Ma bore up bravely, but there was a longing in her eyes as she kissed Sally Anne good-bye, and an expression of deep concern as she pulled Laura close to her, holding her at length before she released her. Marty turned away lest her own tears spill over.

Clark and Marty lingered for a while, sensing how a difficult time in the Grahams' lives had been made even more so, then collected their children and got themselves on home.

"All in all, this was a good day," Marty told Clark, and he nodded his agreement.

Twenty-Nine

Planting

The sun carried more warmth each day, and Marty was very glad to get the children outside into the fresh air. Clark had finished work on the new bedrooms, and Marty had added her own touches with curtains and rugs. They did appreciate the additional areas for work and play. Clark's days began early and ended only when it was too dark to see any longer in the fields he was tilling, and every day more land was ready for the carefully guarded seed that had survived the fire.

Enough grass was now finding its way out of the earth for the three cows to graze. A young calf was in the weaning pen, the second cow was still to calf, and a third would come much later.

One of the sows already had offspring at her side. Missie was especially captivated by the squealing little piglets trying to get their fair share at mealtimes. The sow had not given them as good a litter as they had hoped, bearing only six and losing two, but they thought the second sow might do better. Three of

Marty's eight hens were sitting on eggs. She hoped to replenish the chicken coop again.

The new barn stood straight and strong, a bit larger than its predecessor. As yet it was still unchinked, but that could be done during slack time later in the year. The roof was on and the floor in. It would do as it was until after the crop was in the ground.

Marty was humming one of the new hymns she was learning as she worked on breakfast preparations. Missie had specifically asked for pancakes, and as Marty stirred the batter she remembered those early weeks in this little house when all she knew how to make was pancakes. Then she thought of the two new brides and wondered how they were making out with their cooking responsibilities. She was sure they would do much better, with Ma having trained them well.

Sally Anne was well settled in. She and Jason had driven over one evening to return the saddle horse. Jason's eyes shone with pride as he boasted of how Sally Anne had hung the curtains, spread the rugs, and set her little kitchen in order. She was a right fine cook, too, he went on, and Sally Anne's cheeks had flushed with pleasure. Clark and Marty chuckled about it later. Marty smiled now as she pictured the young couple so content in their love for each other.

Then her thoughts shifted to Laura. How was Laura really doing? she wondered. Clark had seen her recently when he had driven up over the brow of a hill, and there was Laura walking down the road. She had seemed startled at his sudden appearance, he said, and had turned sharply away. When he stopped the team to offer her a lift, she looked back at him to say, "No thanks, walkin' be right good for me." But her eyes looked troubled and there was a bruise on her cheek. He had gone on his way, but as he related his story to Marty that eve-ning she could tell he was deeply troubled by it all. *Poor Laura,* Marty thought, shaking her head. To be expecting a child with this man and seeming so unhappy and alone. Her heart ached for her—and for Ma Graham.

She could hear Clark whistling as he came from the barn, so she called Missie to come quickly to the table. *I wonder,* she thought as she helped the child into her chair, *if spring plantin' always makes a man so happy like.*

Spring was getting into her blood, too, and she was anxious to sink her own hands into the soil. It was so wonderful to feel slim and comfortable again. She felt like she was gliding about, no longer weighted down and clumsy "carrying a young'un everywhere I go," as she had expressed it once to Ma. She was thankful to have baby Clare out where she could hug him close or lay him down at will.

During their morning reading and prayer, Marty almost smiled as Clark read, "'Come unto me, all ye that labour and are heavy laden, and I will give you rest.'" She felt she understood the meaning of Jesus' words in a special way.

I thank ye, Lord, that ye be teachin' me how to rest in you, she prayed inwardly. *Ya be comfortin' me, and I be grateful for that.*

After Clark had finished praying and committing their day to God, Marty asked, "Be it about time to plant the garden?"

"Some of the seeds should go in now. I be thinkin' this mornin' thet I best put the plow to work turnin' the ground. Should be ready fer ya in short order. Ya wantin' to plant it today?"

"Oh yes," Marty answered enthusiastically. "Me, I'm right eager to get goin' on it. Only . . ."

When she couldn't think of how to tell him, Clark urged, "Only what?"

Marty flushed. "Well . . . I never planted before."

"Planted what?"

"Planted anythin'."

"Didn't yer folks have themselves a garden?"

"My ma said 'twas a nuisance, thet she'd as leave buy off a neighbor or from the store. She didn't care none fer the soil, I reckon."

"An' you?"

"I think I'd love to git into makin' somethin' grow. I can hardly wait to try. Only . . ."

Clark looked across at her. "Only what?" he prompted again.

"Well," Marty gulped, "I know thet the garden be a woman's work, but I was wonderin' . . ." She hesitated. "Jest this one time, could ya show me how to plant the seeds an' all?"

Clark looked as though he was trying not to smile and answered slowly, "I reckon I could . . . this once, mind."

Marty looked at him and the twinkle in his eye and took a deep breath of relief. It was the first time she had been able to bring herself to ask him for something, and he seemed to be pleased rather than offended by it. She said, "The best time be right after dinner while the young'uns be havin' their naps. Will the ground be plowed an' ready by then?"

Clark nodded. "I think I can oblige that schedule," he said with mock seriousness as he got up for the coffeepot. Marty nearly choked on a mouthful of pancake. It was the first time she had missed getting his second cup of coffee for some months. Clark seemed unperturbed as he poured for both of them and returned to his place.

Over their steaming mugs they discussed what seeds she would plant; then he reached for his hat. "Thet be good coffee," he said as he went out the door.

At noon after the dinner dishes were done and the children settled, Clark and Marty spread the garden seeds out on the kitchen table to decide what was to be put in at first planting and what left until later. Clark patiently showed her the different seeds, telling her what they were and the peculiarity of their growing habits. Marty listened wide-eyed. He knew so much, Clark did, and as he talked about the seeds, they seemed to take on personalities right before her eyes—like children, needing special care and attention.

They soon gathered up the seeds and headed for the garden. The sun warmed the ground, making the freshly turned soil smell delightfully inviting. The two laughed together about how Missie, and soon Clare, too, would want to be getting their hands—as well as the rest of their little bodies—into the dirt.

Marty reached down and let a handful of the soil trickle through her fingers. *It's beautiful,* she wanted to say, but it seemed such a foolish word to describe dirt. She suddenly stopped, and turning her back to Clark, she slipped off her shoes. Then lifting her skirt modestly, she peeled off her stockings and tucked them carefully into the toes of the shoes. Standing barefoot, feeling the luxury of the warm earth, she dug her toes deeply into its moist richness. She felt like a child again—young and free, with burdens and responsibilities stripped away for the moment.

No wonder horses like ta lie down and roll when their harness is taken off, she thought. *Me, I'd love to be doin' the same thing.*

Clark was already busy preparing rows for her to plant. She

went down on her knees and began to drop seeds into the fertile ground.

"Someday soon, I'll be watchin' ya grow," she said quietly as the tiny carrot seeds spilled from her hand.

Clark returned to cover the row after she had placed the seed.

He looks to be enjoyin' it 'most as much as I am, thought Marty. Then she caught sight of their gamboling calf and wished she herself had the nerve to skip around like that. *It's good jest to be livin' on sech a day.*

The two worked on together, for the most part in silence, and Marty was feeling a new comradeship with the earth and with this tall, patient man whom she called her husband. Nearing the end of their task, Clark squatted down to carefully pat earth over the sweet corn Marty had just dropped into the ground.

Seeing his rather unstable position, Marty sneaked up behind him and gave him a playful shove. He went sprawling in the loose dirt as he took a quick look at her trying to hide her laughter behind her hands.

"Me thinks there's someone askin' fer sweet corn down her neck," he said, scrambling up and reaching for a handful of corn.

Marty was off at a run, but even though she was rather nimble, Clark's long strides soon overtook her. Both long arms went about her, halting her escape. She writhed and twisted against him, seeking to loose herself, but her laughter made her efforts most ineffectual. Clark tried to hold her close so he could free one hand with the corn kernels, but his own laughter was hampering his efforts.

Marty was conscious of his nearness in a way she had never been before. The strength of the arms that held her, the beating of the heart against her cheek, the clean smell of shaving soap that still clung to him—everything about this man who held her sent warm tingles all through her. Her breath was beginning to come in little gasps, and she was powerless to struggle any longer.

The one strong arm pinned her securely against him, and his other hand dumped its load of kernels down the front of her dress. Marty looked up into laughing eyes bent over her, uncomfortably close to her own. The breath caught in her throat as a strangely familiar emotion swept through her. The expression on Clark's face was somehow changing from teasing to something else.

Marty pulled back abruptly, an unreasoning fear filling her heart and her body going weak.

"Thet be Clare?" she said quickly, pushing with trembling hands against Clark's chest.

Clark let her go, and she half ran, half stumbled to the house, her cheeks aflame.

Inside she leaned her head against the bedroom door, trying to sort out the reasons for her throbbing heart and troubled spirit. She could find no answer, and after giving herself several minutes to get herself in hand, she picked up her courage and returned to the garden. But Clark was just putting away the tools. The job was done.

Thirty

Sorrow

Marty looked out the window each morning to check on the progress of the garden. Tiny green stalks were starting to push through, and Missie was nearly as delighted as Marty as they watched them grow. The little girl quickly learned that she should not step on the tender plants or pull them up to inspect their roots.

The activities and conversations in the household seemed to be normal, but deep down Marty knew something had changed. Clark was as considerate as ever, and they still talked things over and enjoyed the children. But there was an uneasy acknowledgment that things were different. She would not let herself think too deeply about it. It was fairly easy to go through the motions of the day in the same orderly fashion she had learned to follow.

She rose early, fed baby Clare, prepared breakfast, and dressed Missie. Then they read Scripture, prayed, and ate the morning meal. She could sit across from Clark, could talk to him and share her plans for the day in as ordinary a way as ever, but she did not let her eyes linger on his for very long. She longed for things to stay as they had been and at the same time feared that they might. *Oh my,* she mourned, *what's happenin'? What's gonna happen . . . ?*

Marty wandered out to the garden to see the growing things and hopefully take her mind off all the perplexing thoughts and feelings. Somehow the garden always gave her a sense of accomplishment and joy. She even found herself talking to the corn, then pushed a little dirt around a potato plant, coaxed the onions and lettuce to hurry a bit, and wondered why she had bothered with so many beans.

She walked over to the fruit trees and was admiring each new leaf when she noted that one of the trees bore blossoms. Her heart leaped—apples. Imagine, apples! Oh, if she could only show Clark, but he was in the fields planting. Then she was surprised to see him coming toward her in long, purposeful strides.

"Clark," she called eagerly. "Clark, come see."

With her eyes fixed on the tree, she reached for his hand to draw him closer.

"Look, Clark," she enthused. "Apple blossoms. We're gonna have apples. Jest look."

There was no answer. She looked up in bewilderment at the silence. Clark stood looking down at her, his face pale, and she could read such sorrow in his eyes. Her heart contracted with fear.

"What . . . what be wrong?" she whispered through trembling lips.

He reached for her then, placing a hand on each shoulder,

and looked deeply at her as though willing her some of his strength to help her bear the news he was bringing.

"It's Laura. They done found her in the crik over by the Conners' cabin."

"Is she . . . is she . . . ?"

"She be dead, Marty."

She sagged against him, her hand pressed to her mouth. "An' Ma?" she finally asked.

"She be needin' ya."

And then she was sobbing, her face against his chest. His hands smoothed her hair as he held her close. She cried for Ma, for Laura, for Ben, even for Sally Anne.

Oh, God, she prayed. *Ya be the only one to be helpin' at a time like this. Help us all now. Please, God, help us now.* Somehow she knew Clark was silently praying the same prayer.

Marty was there when Laura's body was brought to the Grahams'. She would never forget the heartrending scene. Ma gathered the lifeless body into her arms, weeping as though her heart would break and rocking back and forth, saying over and over, "My poor baby, my poor little darlin'." After a time, she wiped her tears, squared her shoulders determinedly, and began to tenderly prepare the body for burial. Ben's grief certainly matched Ma's, but he did not feel the same freedom to express it. Marty had never seen such an ashen face, such bewilderment and grief, as she saw in Ben. She was even more concerned for Ben than for Ma.

Ben insisted on riding over to the Conners' cabin. Unbeknownst to him, Clark had already been there. He had found a

219

very drunk Milt, who swore he knew nothing of Laura's death. He may have roughed her up a bit, he admitted. But she was quite alive when he'd last seen her, he insisted. Clark had convinced Milt in no uncertain terms that he would be wise to move farther west and to do so immediately.

Clark rode over again with Ben, making no mention of his previous visit. The cabin looked to be deserted for good and in a great hurry. Clark told Marty later that he was very relieved Milt had already gone, fearing what Ben might have done in his present state.

Neighbors came, and they lovingly set to work. The coffin was built and the grave dug, and the frail body of the girl was committed to the ground. In the absence of a preacher, Clark was asked to say the "buryin' words." Marty could sense how difficult it was for him as he held the Bible open and read the ancient words, "'For dust thou art, and unto dust thou shalt return. . . .'"

Solemnly they all turned from the new mound, leaving Ma and Ben to sort out and adjust to their grief. Ma, whose wisdom and care had comforted many a neighbor in tragic circumstances, once again said through her tears that time was the answer. This time she was saying it to herself.

Thirty-One

New Strength

By June the second cow had calved and, to Clark's great surprise, bore twin female calves—a special gift from God, he announced. "We sure be able to make use o' one more," he told Marty. He was carrying Clare, and Marty held firmly to Missie's hand as they watched the calves awkwardly trying to stand up. Missie thought it was quite funny and would have loved to climb in the pen with them.

A week later the other sow had her pigs, not an exceptional litter but an acceptable one, and she had kept all eight of them.

The hatching of the chicks meant three proud mothers were strutting around with a total of twenty-seven chicks fluttering between them. Missie was quite insistent that the chicks would want to be held, but fortunately they were able to keep away from her chubby hands.

Marty still had not been able to shake off the sorrow of Laura's tragic death. It seemed to hang about her, choking out the happiness she wanted to feel.

Missie came down with the measles, and even though she was not awfully sick, Marty hovered over her, worried lest another tragedy strike. But the child was rather quickly up and around again, pretending that her doll had the measles "an' needs a wet cloth on her head, too."

It was while Missie was still red-blotched and feverish that news came of the first wagon train passing through town, heading east. Marty was busy with doctoring Missie, and there would be other trains, she told herself.

On a warm June day after Missie was back to health, Marty tucked the two youngsters in for their afternoon nap and decided to step outside for a breath of fresh air. She had been cooped up long enough and felt rather restless and uneasy.

She walked through her much-loved garden, noticing how much the plants had grown during the time of Missie's illness. The blossoms on the apple tree had dropped their petals, making room for the fruit forming on the branches.

She walked past the buildings and down to the stream. She seemed drawn to that quiet spot she had discovered long ago when she had needed comfort—then because of her own loss, and now because of Ma's.

She really needed a place to think, to sort things out. Life was so confusing—the good mixed with the bad; such a strange combination of happiness and sorrow.

She sat leaning against a tree trunk, watching the clear water gurgling by.

"God," she whispered, "what be it all about? I don't understand much 'bout ya. I do know thet yer good. I know thet ya love me, thet ya died for me; but I don't understand 'bout losin', 'bout the pain thet goes so deep I can't see the end. I don't understand at all."

She closed her eyes, feeling the strength of the sturdy tree trunk behind her, listening to the rustling of the leaves, feeling the slight breeze ruffling her hair.

She closed her eyes more tightly, drawing from the peace and beauty of the woods. When she opened them, Clark was there, leaning against another tree, his eyes on her face.

She was startled at first and quickly stood.

"Sorry to be frightin' ya," he told her. "I seed ya comin' over here, an' I thought ya'd maybe not mind me joinin' ya."

"'Course not."

Silence fell between them. Clark picked up a branch and broke off small pieces. Marty watched the stream carry them swirling away in the current.

"Guess life be somethin' like thet stream," Clark commented quietly.

"Meanin'?"

"Things happen. Leaves fill it up—animals waller in it—spring floods fill it with mud." He hesitated. "Bright sunshine makes it like a mirror glass; sparklin' rain makes it grow wider, but it still moves on—unchangin' like—the same stream even with all the things thet happen to it. It breaks through the leaves, it clears itself of the animal wallerin'—the muddy waters turn clean agin. The sunshine an' the rain it accepts, fer they give life an' strengthen it like, but it really could have done without 'em. They're extries like." He broke another branch and added more to the stream.

"Life's like thet," he picked up again. "Bad things come, but life keeps on flowin', clearin' its path gradual like, easin' its own burden. The good times come, too; we maybe could make it without 'em, but the Lord knows we need 'em to help give meanin'—to strengthen us, to help us reflect the sunshine.

"Guess one has to 'spect the good an' the bad, long as we be livin', an' try one's best to make the bad hurt as little as possible, an' the good—one has to help it grow like, make all the good things count."

Marty had shut her eyes again as Clark was speaking. She stood there now, eyes closed, breathing deeply of the woods and the stream.

Life was like that stream. It went on, whatever happened to it. She was ready to go on now, too. She had drawn strength from the woods. No, not that. She had drawn strength from the God who had made the woods.

Thirty-Two

Love Comes Softly

Marty hurried through her mending, wanting to have it all finished before she had to get supper ready. She was working on a pair of Clark's overalls, the last item in her mending basket. As she handled the garment, she was reminded again of what a big man she was married to.

"Why, they'd swaller me," she chuckled as she held them up in front of her. Missie thought it was funny, too.

Missie was trying to copy her mama in everything she did. Marty had given her a scrap of cloth and a button. She threaded a blunt needle for Missie and showed the little girl the art of button sewing.

"Ya may as well learn how it be done," she told her. "Ya'll need to be knowin' how to do this afore we know it."

Missie busied herself pushing the needle in and out of the material. Marty smiled at the child's efforts—the thread showed up in some very strange places, but Missie was quite happy with her newly learned skill.

Baby Clare lay on a rug, cooing and talking to himself and anyone else who would care to listen. He was four months old now, a bright, happy, healthy child, who as yet had not fulfilled Clark's dire predictions of "wait until the teeth come in." All three of his family members doted on him, so why shouldn't he be content?

Missie talked to him as she worked. "See, baby. See big si'ter. She sewin'. Do ya like it? Look, Mama. He smiles. Clare likes it—my sewin'."

Marty nodded at them both and went on sewing the overall patch. A loud crash made her jump and Missie exclaimed, "Dad-burn!" as she looked at the spilled button box.

"Missie, ya mustn't say thet."

Missie stared up at her mama. "You did."

"Well, I don't say it anymore, an' I don't want ya sayin' it, either. Now, let's git down an' pick up all them buttons on the floor 'fore Clare gits 'em in his mouth." Missie obeyed, helping put the buttons back in their container and placing it on the sewing machine.

Marty finished her patch and hurried to get supper ready. Clark would be in shortly from chores, and she planned to talk with him about moving the children's beds to their new bedroom. This would give her a bit more space to move around in her own small bedroom. Clark had moved his things into the other one just as soon as he'd been able to get a roof over it and the floor in. With Clare sleeping through the night now and the warmer weather, Marty didn't need to worry about the children becoming uncovered. It would be nice to be able to reach her things without banging her shins on a small bed or tripping over Missie's doll.

She almost had the meal on the table when Missie came flying through the door.

"Mama—Mama—Clare sick!"

"Whatcha meanin'?" Marty spun around to look at her.

The child grabbed her hand, jerking her toward the sitting room.

"He sick!" she screamed.

Marty ran toward the rasping, gurgling sound.

She snatched up the baby, who was struggling furiously, his little fists flailing the air as he fought for breath.

"He's chokin'!" Marty cried. She turned him upside down and smacked him on the back between his tiny shoulder blades.

Clare still struggled.

"Run fer yer pa," Marty told the small child, trying to keep the panic out of her voice. Missie ran.

Marty reversed the baby and carefully pushed a finger down his throat. She thought she could feel something, but the end of her finger just ticked it. Clare was gagging, but nothing came up.

Clark came running through the door, his eyes wild with concern.

"He's chokin'!" Marty told him.

"Slap his back."

"I did." Marty was in tears now.

"Put yer finger—"

"I tried."

"I'll git the doc."

"There's no time."

"Wrap 'im up," Clark instructed her, his voice firm. "I'll git the horses."

The baby was still breathing—struggling, gasping little breaths, but he was still breathing.

"Oh, God," Marty prayed desperately. "Please help us. Please help us. Jest keep 'im breathin' 'til we reach the doc."

She grabbed a blanket and wrapped it about Clare. Missie stood, eyes wide, too frightened to even cry.

"Missie, git yer coat on," Marty ordered, "an' bring a blanket from yer bed so thet ya can lay down in the wagon."

The child hurried to obey.

Clark raced the team toward the house. Marty ran forward with the baby in her arms and Missie by the hand. Without speaking, Clark hauled Missie up, putting her and her blanket in a safe place on the wagon floor; then he helped Marty and the baby over the wheel, and they were off.

The long trip to town was a nightmare. The ragged breathing of the baby was broken only by his fits of coughing. The horses plunged on, harness creaking as sweat flecked their necks and haunches. Clark urged them on and on. Marty clung to Clare; the wagon jostled her bones, sweat from the horses dotting her arms and face.

We'll never make it—we'll never make it, Marty cried inwardly as Clare's gasping breath seemed to be weakening and the horses' breakneck speed slackened. But on they galloped, seeming to draw on a reserve Marty would have never guessed they had.

The baby's breathing was even more erratic as lights from the town finally came into view. Clark spoke again to the horses and they sped forward. How could they continue on at this pace? They must be ready to fall in the harness, but Clark's coaxing voice seemed to strengthen them.

Straight to the doctor's they galloped, and Clark pulled the heaving horses to a stop and jumped down before the wagon had stopped rolling. He reached up for little Clare, and Marty surrendered him, watching Clark head for the door on the run. Marty turned to help Missie up from the floor of the wagon. For a moment Marty clung to the little girl, wanting to assure her that all would be well—but would it? She climbed over the wheel and held up her arms for the child.

By the time Marty entered the room that served as the doctor's office, the baby had been placed on a small table under, what seemed to her, a very bright light. The doctor was bending over him, appearing to completely overwhelm the small gasping figure as he examined him.

"He has a tiny object stuck in his throat," he said matter-of-factly, just as though Marty's whole world did not revolve around that very fact.

"I'm going to have to go after it. We'll have to put him to sleep. Call my missus, will you? She helps with this—has special training."

Clark rapped loudly on the door separating the office from the living quarters, and a woman came into the room. On seeing the small baby fighting for every breath, her eyes showed instant concern.

"Oh my! What's his problem?"

"He has something in his throat. We're going to have to put him to sleep and remove it."

The doctor was already in action as he spoke, and she quickly joined him, the two working as a well-matched team.

The doctor seemed to have forgotten the rest of the family as he hurriedly prepared himself; then he looked up suddenly.

"You folks can just take a chair in our living room. This won't take long, but we work best alone."

Clark took Marty's arm and led her from the room. She went reluctantly, hating to leave the precious little baby, fearing every breath might be his last.

Clark helped ease her numb body into a chair. She was still clinging to Missie. He suggested that Missie could sit on another chair beside her, but she shook her head. Clark himself did not sit down but paced the floor with an anxious face. Marty knew he was petitioning his God. His hand trembled as he removed the hat he had forgotten. Watching him, Marty realized just how much he loved the wee baby. *He loves him as though he were his own,* she thought and didn't find this strange at all. After all, she loved Missie in the same way and had as good as forgotten there ever was a time when the little girl had been only a tiny stranger.

Centuries seemed to drag by, and Missie finally wriggled out of Marty's arms and fell asleep on her blanket in a corner. But eventually the doctor appeared at the door. Clark crossed to Marty, placing a hand on her shoulder as if to protect her from hearing the worst, but the doctor smiled at them.

"Well, Mr. Davis," he said, looking at Clark, who was, after all, the one responsible for his coming to this town. "Your boy is going to be just fine. Had this button lodged in his throat; luckily it was turned sideways or—"

"It weren't luck," Clark responded.

"Call it what you may"—the doctor shrugged—"it's out now. You can see him if you wish."

Marty stood up. *He is all right. My baby is all right.* She wasn't sure her legs could hold her upright. "Oh, God, he's all right. Thank ya. Thank ya!" she exclaimed.

If it hadn't been for Clark's arms about her, she would have gone down in a heap. He pulled her to him, and they wept in thankfulness together.

Clark and Marty stood looking down at the relaxed but pale little face, relief flooding through them. Marty had not released Clark's hand and his arm still steadied her.

"He's been through a lot, poor little fellow," the doctor said sympathetically, and Marty felt she would be forever beholden to this kindly man.

"He needs a long, restful sleep now," the doctor said. "He's still under the effect of the sleeping draught we gave him. I expect he'll sleep through the night without stirring. My wife and I will take turns sitting with him. You folks had best try to get some rest. I'm sure the hotel across the street will have a room."

"Shouldn't . . . shouldn't we stay with 'im?" Marty finally found her voice.

"No need, ma'am," the doctor answered. "He'll sleep, and seems to me you could be using some yourself."

"He's right," Clark said. "Ya be needin' some rest—an' some supper, too. Come on. Let's get across to the hotel."

With a last glance at the sleeping baby, stroking his cheek to assure herself that he was really all right, Marty allowed herself to be led out. Clark picked up the tired and hungry Missie and carried her across the street.

Marty was glad to sink into the chair and hold Missie close, crooning words of love to her, while Clark made arrangements at the desk.

Clark returned to her. "They'll rustle up some supper an' then show ya to a room."

"What 'bout you?"

"I'll be needin' to care fer the horses. They need a good rub-down an' a bit of special care."

Marty nodded. Right now she dearly loved old Dan and Charlie.

"We'll wait fer ya," she nodded.

"Be no need—" Clark started.

"Yes, we'll want to wait for ya."

Clark agreed and went out. While he was gone, Marty told Missie what a brave girl she had been, and how she had helped baby Clare by calling her mama and getting her pa, and lying still on the wagon floor and not crying at the doctor's. She was a big girl and her mama loved her very much.

To Marty's bewilderment, large tears filled Missie's eyes and she began to cry.

At Marty's prompting, she finally sobbed, "But . . . I spill . . . buttons."

Marty pulled her close, rocking her gently. "Missie, Missie, it weren't yer fault that baby Clare found a button thet got missed in our pickin' up. It jest happened, thet's all. Don't ya be frettin' 'bout it. Mama an' yer pa love ya so very much, an' you was a brave girl to be so good. You hush ya, now."

She finally got the little girl comforted.

Clark returned, reporting that Dan and Charlie would be fine after a good rest. And they'd get it, too, he declared—they'd earned it.

The three went in together to the hotel dining room. But none of them felt much like eating. Missie was too tired, Marty too spent, and Clark too relieved to be much interested in food.

After making an effort to down a light meal, they requested that they be shown to their room.

A small cot had been placed in one corner, and the first thing Marty did was prepare Missie for bed as best she could. There was no soft, warm nightie, but Missie didn't mind. She fell asleep almost before she finished her short prayer.

Marty sat beside her until she was sure the child was asleep, then kissed her again and went over to a very weary Clark, who was trying to relax in a large chair.

What could she say to this man who sat before her? This man who comforted her when she sorrowed, understood her joys, gave her strength when her own strength was spent, shared with her his faith, and introduced her to his God. There was so much she felt. That strange, deep stirring within her—she understood it now. It was a longing for this man, his love. She wanted him; she knew that now. But how . . . how could she tell him?

She stood there mute, wanting to say it all, but no words came. Then he rose and reached for his hat.

"Where ya be headin'?" She found her voice then.

"I'm thinkin' thet I'll spend me the night over at the doc's. Iffen little Clare be wakin', I'm thinkin' thet he should wake to some of his own 'stead of strangers."

"But Doc says he won't wake till morn."

"Maybe so. All the same, I'll find comfort jest watchin' him sleep peaceful like. I'll be over in the mornin' to be sure ya not be needin' anythin'."

He turned to go, but she knew she mustn't let him. If he went now without knowing . . .

Still her voice would not obey her command. She reached out and took his sleeve. He turned to her. She could only look at him, imploring him to read in her eyes what she could not say with her lips.

He looked into her face searchingly; then he stepped closer and his hands went to her shoulders, drawing her toward him.

He must have read there what she wanted him to see, but still he hesitated a moment.

"Ya bein' sure?" he asked quietly.

She nodded her head, looking deep into his eyes, and then she was in his arms, being held the way she ached to be held, feeling the strength of his body tight against her, raising trembling lips to his.

How long had she wanted this? She wasn't sure. She only knew that now it seemed like forever. She loved him so much. She must later find the words to tell him so, but for now she would content herself with being held close, hearing his words of love whispered tenderly against her hair.

How did it all come about—this miracle of love? She didn't know. It had come upon her unawares . . . softly.

About the Author

JANETTE OKE was born in Champion, Alberta, to a Canadian prairie farmer and his wife, and she grew up in a large family full of laughter and love. She is a graduate of Mountain View Bible College in Alberta, where she met her husband, Edward. After marrying in 1957, they pastored churches in Indiana and Canada and raised a daughter and three sons. Janette began writing for publication in the late 1970s, and she and Edward eventually moved to Calgary, where Edward served in several positions on college faculties while she wrote.

Janette is credited with launching the modern era of inspirational fiction with the publication of her first novel, *Love Comes Softly*, in 1979. She has gone on to write or cowrite more than fifty novels, as well as numerous stories for children. More than thirty million copies of her books have been sold to date, and several of her books have been adapted for film and television.

Celebrated for her significant contribution to Christian literature, Janette is the recipient of the ECPA President's Award, the CBA Life Impact Award, the Gold Medallion, and the Christy Award for Excellence in Fiction.

Janette and Edward make their home in Alberta, Canada.

More from Janette Oke

Janette Oke's beloved LOVE COMES SOFTLY series is a reassuring picture of how God's love can deepen the affection between two people during times of joy and suffering. Join the multitudes who have laughed, wept, and rejoiced with the Davis family through these gentle prairie love stories.

LOVE COMES SOFTLY: *Love Comes Softly, Love's Enduring Promise, Love's Long Journey, Love's Abiding Joy, Love's Unending Legacy, Love's Unfolding Dream, Love Takes Wing, Love Finds a Home*

Life is changing for young Joshua Chadwick Jones. In SEASONS OF THE HEART, he learns to grow and love in the midst of loss and disappointment. A poignant tale of the power of faith shaping a life in a small prairie community.

SEASONS OF THE HEART: *Once Upon a Summer, The Winds of Autumn, Winter Is Not Forever, Spring's Gentle Promise*

You May Also Like . . .

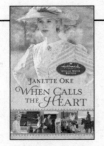

Nothing in her cultured upbringing prepared Elizabeth for her teaching position in the Canadian West. Is her faith sufficient to sustain her through the rigors of life on the frontier? Will she find love in this remote place . . . or weather her trials alone?

CANADIAN WEST: *When Calls the Heart, When Comes the Spring, When Breaks the Dawn, When Hope Springs New, Beyond the Gathering Storm, When Tomorrow Comes*
by Janette Oke

Beth Thatcher has lived a privileged life. Now, inspired by her aunt Elizabeth, Beth has accepted a teaching position in the rugged foothills of Canada. There, her courage—and her heart—will be tested in unexpected ways.

RETURN TO THE CANADIAN WEST: *Where Courage Calls, Where Trust Lies, Where Hope Prevails*
by Janette Oke and Laurel Oke Logan

◊BETHANYHOUSE